I0733352

LIMELIGHT

LIMELIGHT

E. DAVIES

HeartEyes Press

Copyright © 2021 by E. Davies

All rights reserved.

This book was inspired by the True North Series written by Sarina Bowen. It is an original work that is published by Heart Eyes Press LLC.

No part of this book may be reproduced in any form or by any electronic or mechanical means, including information storage and retrieval systems, without written permission from the author, except for the use of brief quotations in a book review.

TAG

"Who's a thirsty little guy? Yeah… me too. That's life, buddy."

I hang up my clipboard and pat the side of the stainless steel fermenter that holds sixty gallons of my newest batch of mead.

Everyone warned me about moving to the woods of Vermont to start my own business. Well, not so much *warned* as *looked at me like I had six heads*. Maybe they were right. Out here on my own, I'm finally going crazy.

At least the job suits me, though it's a far cry from my former life. I traded the limelight for a beard and a bunch of beehives, and I make mead from my honey. Running a business is a full-time job and a half, but it's all my own. Nobody can throw me out or keep me down.

What I didn't consider before my wilderness move is the number of eligible men who want to be swept off their feet and carted away in my white pickup truck for a happy-ever-after farming life.

To be precise, so far that number is zero. I'll keep hoping for a miracle.

The skitter of claws and a soft whine from outside make me smile. I'm not *completely* alone. Queenie, my chocolate Lab, has enough energy for both of us. Great when I'm out hiking, but I feel guilty when she's ready to hop in the truck and I can't bring her along.

"Sorry, girl," I call out, hoisting a case of mead on each shoulder. "Not tonight."

I carefully do the one-two step it requires to keep a huge, curious, overgrown puppy out of the food production area she really shouldn't be in.

Today, I manage it. Queenie takes one look at what I'm carrying and spins in a circle, wagging her tail furiously like she hopes that will convince me. Sometimes her cute act works. If it's gonna be a quick drop-and-go, I'll bring her and let her sit in the truck.

But with the nights getting chilly, I don't want her stuck out there waiting for me... not that I can enjoy a late night. I have to feed the mead again at midnight.

No point in getting dressed up for an evening off, then. This red plaid shirt and jeans will do fine for a quick delivery. I'm bringing these cases to Vino and Veritas, the local bookstore and wine bar. Here in Burlington, people aren't pretentious. I won't have to sneak in the back door... so to speak.

I drop off the cases in my truck, and then close the door before Queenie can jump in. She puts on her best dejected face as I lead her to the house.

"I can't smuggle you in tonight," I tell her, scratching the top of her head before I push open the door and wait for her to scamper inside first. "You wouldn't fit in my handbag. Should have thought about that before you grew so much, huh?"

Queenie's big even for a Lab. It means I can't keep food on the counters. She can pretty much barge into any room she chooses, and often does, even when I'm showering. But it takes a forceful personality to be around me. I love her to death. She's my best girl.

And right now, butter wouldn't melt in her mouth as she gazes at me expectantly.

"Okay, okay," I laugh, my willpower lasting about two

seconds. I open the cupboard, and before I can even grab the jar of dog treats inside, she does her happy dance around my ankles.

"Sit," I tell her firmly, biting back my smile and waiting. When she gets her excitement under control enough to put her butt on the ground, I toss her two treats, both of which she snatches out of the air like a champ. "Attagirl. Go take a nap."

Queenie can be obedient when she chooses. She skitters across the hardwood floor of the old farmhouse to curl up in her giant, fluffy dog bed in front of the fireplace.

It's getting cold enough at night to light the wood stove in the evenings. There's nothing I love more than sitting in front of it with Queenie sprawled across my lap. Together, we watch the flames and daydream.

In the last four years, I've settled into a seasonal rhythm, and this time of year is the best. I've just finished the hard work of prepping the beehives for winter. My only stress is starting new batches. Once the mead is aging, I've got a lot more time to myself.

Not gonna lie, though. The evenings are long when the only soul around speaks in woofs and barks, not English. Once upon a time, in the bright lights of the city, I could have found a friendly face and warm bed any time I chose.

I don't miss the attention, but now and then I wonder how my life could have played out differently.

"Oh, stop moping," I grumble. I'm no longer Titus Taylor, rock star and media darling set firmly on a rising trajectory to superstardom. It feels so long ago that it might as well have been another life.

I'm not exactly in hiding, but I haven't told anyone here who I used to be. I'd rather blend in than step into another spotlight, or worse yet, make people think I'm some big-headed star. That's not me. Not anymore.

I'm just Tag now. A guy with a delivery to make and a dog to cuddle later.

After shrugging on my insulated flannel jacket, I hop in my truck for the quick drive to the town center.

Parking is easy to find in the side street near Vino and Veritas. After shoving the truck door closed, I hoist both cases of mead bottles into my arms and head for the front door.

Live music greets me, stopping me in my tracks for a moment. Did I miss a concert? No, wait. Duh. It's Sunday: open mic night.

There's a spotlight on the stage, where a young guy is just finishing a song on his guitar to a round of applause. I duck my head and steer around the crowd. Once I get to the bar, I jerk my chin up in a greeting to the bartender, Murph.

"Evening, Tag," he greets me. He's wearing a black shirt with pink writing and a sparkly necklace, and a charming grin as usual.

"Going well?" I jerk my head toward the stage.

"Can't beat the talent here in Burlington. You still living under a rock?" His teasing is always kind, like he wants to encourage me to get out more, and it makes me smile.

"Business keeps me busy," I say, but heat creeps up my cheeks. Guilty as charged. To hide my blush, I quickly look across the room again.

I might stay for a few minutes. God knows I've heard some off-key singing in my life. *Done* some off-key singing, in the early days. I don't mind that.

As long as nobody ropes me into going up to the mic. Thankfully, Vino and Veritas plays more jazz than pop rock music, but someone with a keen ear could recognize me in a flash.

I've avoided any kind of publicity and moved here under a new name. For the last few years, I've stuck to myself and let everyone assume I'm a shy wallflower. Okay, I guess what I'm doing here in Vermont *could* technically be called hiding out.

My gaze lands on one particular face in the crowd, and then I can't look away.

A guy around my age is standing by the wall, shuffling papers in his hands. He looks like he expects a tiger to jump out of the crowd and swallow him whole.

He's cute, though. Really cute. A head full of defined gold curls, thin eyebrows, full lips, a scruffy jawline that could kill a man. He's dressed up nicely too, in dark slacks and a white shirt that clings to his shoulders, hinting at biceps and pecs that I wouldn't mind getting up close and personal with.

My heart skips a beat or three.

"Who's up next? Him?"

Murph follows my gaze. "Yeah. He's reading poetry, I think."

Then someone comes up to the bar and Murph excuses himself, so I nod absently. My gaze is fixed on the poet.

Is he…?

No, there's no point in even wondering if the guy is single and interested in reclusive hermits. He's gorgeous. He'll be mobbed by fans.

I lean on the bar and watch, trying to behave myself and not mentally undress the poor stranger. Apparently it's been *way* longer than I realized.

Tap tap. The guy taps the microphone to make sure it's live. I wince, but mercifully there's no feedback. He leans in, his eyes skittering across the room like he doesn't know where to look. "H-Hi," he stutters. "I'm Caleb. Uh, I'll just… um…"

Caleb almost drops his papers as he fumbles to take the mic out of the stand. I shove my hands in my pockets and fix a supportive smile on my face in case he happens to look my way.

I know what a difference it makes, seeing smiles instead of folded arms.

When Caleb has the microphone gripped deathly tight in one hand, he looks at his papers and comes to the same conclusion I already did—he can't hold it and turn pages.

"Sorry." He gulps and shoves the mic back into the stand, raising the papers until they form a shield in front of his chest. At least he doesn't go totally amateur and raise them so high we can't see his face.

Yeah, textbook stage fright. Poor guy.

"Oh, uh, I should say, I'm reading poetry. My poems. Hope you like them." His voice is light, musical, and warm despite the taut, breathy stress in it. There's a faint, stereotypical lisp to his words, too, but he hardly seems conscious of it.

Just relax. You've got this, I urge like I'm coaching Super Bowl players on TV.

"Okay, um. Here goes..."

Caleb stares at the paper like he hopes it will save him, and then launches into a poem.

"Your sheets, a cold rip—rippling mountain..." He gulps for breath, sneaks a panicked look over the page, and his voice turns strangled. "*Range,*" he continues with determination, like he's trying to murder someone with his syllables. "Brushed by dawn."

Then he stops again, gripping both sides of the stack of paper so tightly I'm afraid he's going to rip them in two.

I can't watch any longer. Caleb looks like he might cry. It's been years since I've felt the dizzying panic of stage fright myself, but seeing his face makes me feel like it was yesterday.

I'd tear down the stage barehanded to rescue him.

I step away from the bar and stride through the room, picking my way to the little table at the front of the room. Then I sit and smile up at him.

Caleb's eyes go wide as he looks at me like he's praying for the stage to open up and swallow him whole.

When I have his gaze, my heart skips another beat, and my fingertips suddenly go all tingly. Like I'm the one in the spotlight, not him. From up here, I can see each gold strand of his curls and the taut line of his mouth.

I gesture with two fingers to my eyes, then point at myself. Then I wave my finger in a circle and mouth, *Start again.*

If he can just look at me and only me, he can get through this.

My first time in an arena of two thousand people, I played the whole show to a woman who looked kind of like my mom and was obviously there with her daughter. They probably never even knew they got a private concert.

Caleb blinks several times, but he fixes his gaze on me, nods, and then looks down at the page again. Then he lowers the papers and speaks from memory.

His voice flows, and the words suddenly spark to life.

> *Your sheets, a cold rippling mountain*
> *range brushed by dawn. Plucked*
> *from the bed, the peaks overshadow*
> *your body far below, a winding river,*
> *still and clear. From the summit*
> *I look down upon the view again,*
> *again, nursing parched fingertips.*
> *One step to water's edge, but*
> *how far could I bear to fall?*

Caleb never looks away from me. His eyes sparkle with suddenly lively, even playful energy. Holy shit, I feel like I'm the center of his universe, and I *love* it.

Like we're the only two people in the room, the rest of the world falls away. My smile fades into intense focus. I don't want to miss a word. I wish I could replay these few seconds over and over later for, uh, *reasons*.

I'm not being serenaded, I try to remind myself. *For god's sake, Tag. He's just looking at me. He's not talking* to *me*.

I wish he were. Like a punch in the gut, I feel the yearning in his words. It floats from his voice to my ears and burrows deep into my belly where it's suddenly mine, too.

I can barely breathe with it. My throat is tight with loneliness and a bittersweet tang of memory. He caught me on a lonely night, that's all.

I swallow down the feelings and bring my palms together. The others watching join in for a few moments in a soft ripple of applause. The murmurs of conversation behind me are low and respectful.

For the first time, Caleb smiles in a flash of white teeth, youthful exuberance and relief shining from his face. I might as well have been turned to stone. I'm transfixed, completely under his spell.

One at a time, from memory, he reads the other four poems he brought tonight. They're pretty, too. Lots of nature references. One quirky poem about numbers. I like the one about an old house, too.

But they don't stick in my mind and gut and make a home in me like that first one. My heart is still fluttering at a mile a minute.

Then it hits me: after he's done, this guy is probably going to talk to me. He's going to want to know who I am and how I knew how to deal with stage fright.

Eventually he might ask questions, and then I'll have to answer them, and those piercing eyes will stick me to the spot and carve my standoffish mask to pieces.

And… I don't hate that idea.

Oh, no.

I haven't felt these butterflies in my stomach about anyone for a good couple of years. Haven't tried to date anyone in even longer. I usually keep my distance and let the feelings pass.

But it's too late for that. Caleb's on his last sheet of paper, while all rational thought is quickly slipping out of my grasp. Instead, a shimmer of pleasure dances over my skin when he smiles at me.

I can't run this time. But I'm going to try—I just know it. Because at the end of the day, that's who I am.

CALEB

My quarter-life crisis showed up a year late.

Nothing else could explain me coming to Vino and Veritas on open mic night, let alone *voluntarily* stepping into the spotlight.

Get me one-on-one and I'm bubbly, but in front of a crowd? Nope. I'm not that guy. I never have been, and now I'm even more sure I never will be. I'm the timid wallflower at yoga class, an office party, or—most of all—a stage.

The hell was I thinking?

Thank God for Angel. I don't know his name, so that's what I'm calling him in my head—the guy who swooped in from nowhere to save me.

When I practiced reading my poetry in front of the mirror, there was nobody watching me. But up here, the wave of paralyzing dread just floored me. I was about half a second from running off the stage and never showing my face in Vino and Veritas again.

But then Angel showed up. With a few simple gestures, he coached me through the fear like it was nothing. I didn't think it would work, focusing on one person alone, but I was desperate.

And then... the rest of the room disappeared, and for the past fifteen minutes, nothing has existed except Angel and me. He watches me attentively, his head tilted slightly.

I can talk to him like an old friend. I just let the words engraved in my head from weeks of lunch break rehearsals flow from my lips.

But I'm drawing a blank right now, instinctively reaching for more words in my brain and shuffling the papers in my hands.

I come up blank. That was it. The five I've prepared are all over. Time just… vanished. I'm coming to, like waking after a strange accidental nap. The world is watching again.

I've already done my thing. I don't need to panic now. It's over. I did it. And I'm still alive!

Without the words to focus on, I can't help staring at Angel. He's gorgeous. I noticed as he walked up to the stage that he's a little broader and taller than me. His clothes aren't meant to be form-fitting, yet muscles fill out his plaid shirt sleeves and trouser legs.

Angel has a close-trimmed beard that obscures his jaw, but his lips are full and pink, and his dark eyes sparkle.

This is the kind of guy I've always fantasized about. Usually while standing against the wall of the bar, torn asunder between two hopes. On the one hand, hoping he doesn't look—or worse yet, *talk* to me. On the other, desperately needing him to and inevitably being disappointed when he doesn't.

"Uh, that… that was my last one." I stare down at the papers in my hands and then bob my head in a quick, nervous half-bow, half-nod, entirely-awkward thing.

The applause that greets me is polite and steady. Not scattered, and certainly not rapturous. The way you clap when you didn't hate something but you're glad it's over.

Did I suck that much?

I swallow the lump in my throat and focus again on Angel. He's the only one applauding hard. I can't bear to see the disappointment in his face when he looks around and realizes that nobody else was that impressed.

There are no prizes for surviving, like my brothers would say. *Only winning.*

And I sure as hell didn't win.

I turn away and clatter down the steps at the side of the stage. Embarrassment uncoils in my gut and tightens like a snake around my throat. I should just go home now and sleep for twelve hours before work tomorrow and pretend none of this ever happened.

My brothers will rib me for days when they hear about this— and no doubt they will.

"Well done," one older lesbian couple tells me, waving me over to their small table. They're leaning on it with drinks and sympathetic smiles.

I manage a smile for them and mumble my thanks, but I can't resist a peek over my shoulder. A peek at *him*.

When I turn back to the couple, one of the women winks at me. "Better go catch your boyfriend before he leaves."

"What?" I spin around again, my cheeks burning at the word. "He's not—I mean—I don't—"

There's Angel, skulking away between the tables. I could swear he's trying to sneak to the exit.

Despite my performance, I want to talk to him. Thank him for rescuing me. Yeah, those are excuses. He's hot and he seemed genuine, and I don't want him to leave.

If he walks out, I might never see him again. That thought is worse than the thought of screwing up the courage to approach.

I nod an embarrassed thanks to the women. Then I hurry in between the tables to cut off my hunky savior. With panic in my throat, I reach for words—any words—that would stop him from leaving.

"I think you're supposed to leave behind a glass slipper."

Oh, God. Why was *that* the first thing out of my mouth? My cheeks flush with scorching heat, and I kind of want to disappear into the ground. I should have apologized for making him stay to listen to everything, or thanked him, or said something *normal*.

The guy stops, though. I can hardly breathe as he turns and slowly raises an eyebrow, an amused smile curving his sensual lips. Straight away, my gaze slides down to his feet before I manage to look him in the eye again.

I just stared at him for ten minutes. Why is it so much harder to make eye contact one-on-one?

"I figured you'd have enough dances on your card tonight." My Angel's voice is a slow and sensual rumble. Like a hug that lasts long enough to make my heart sing.

"Oh, I... I'm not really the dancing type?" My laugh as I say it makes the last few words breathy and indecisive, and I kick myself. He's clearly drawn to confidence. The moment my newly-discovered stage persona switched off—he left.

Be strong. Be confident, I urge myself, but I just want to melt into a puddle of goo at Angel's feet.

"Can I thank you with a glass of wine or a mojito or a beer or, uh..." I gulp for breath. "The drink of your choice? Please?"

My self-kicking intensifies. *Almost smooth, except for all the words that weren't.*

But despite my fears, Angel smiles back at me. It lights up his whole face, crinkling the corners of his eyes gently. "How can I say no?"

"Because I'm a complete nerd and I just froze up on stage and nearly peed my pants because, like, ten people looked at me at the same time?"

I grin at him so he doesn't try to reassure me it wasn't that bad. It was, and there's no point in pretending otherwise. I am who I am, even if that's not his thing.

Okay, fine. I'll be briefly and intensely devastated if I'm not his thing. But I'm not going to pretend to be Mr. Slick just to impress him. That way lies misery.

Angel's look is gently amused, even understanding. "What if I'm into shy nerds?"

"*Oh.*" Harnessing my sigh of relief would have powered the whole town for a few seconds. "Then... why run away?"

Angel pauses and scrubs a palm along his scruffy jawline. When he answers, his voice is measured but tentative. "I'm not sure. It's been so long since I felt that kind of spark with anyone. It took me by surprise, I guess." Then he leans in, like he's confiding in me, and I sway toward him too until the scent of his cologne fills my nose. "If anything, I'm the scaredy-cat here."

My heart is pounding and my head spins. I straighten up again. "How about we both pretend to be brave for just one drink, then?" My voice squeaks a little on the very last word, and he pretends not to notice.

"One drink," he agrees, that warm smile returning. "It's a deal." Then he walks alongside me to the bar.

I'm trying to work out how to stand there without hopping from foot to foot with excitement when Murph comes over.

"What can I get you?"

"A mojito, please," I tell him, glancing sideways at Angel to see his reaction. He doesn't roll his eyes or frown or even look vaguely annoyed, though.

Phew. A lot of guys I'm trying to flirt with get uptight about shit like that. And that's when I excuse myself to go "talk to a friend" and they become stories to tell my yoga class.

Murph nods. "And you, Tag?"

"Just a glass of red is fine. Thanks, Murph."

That must be Angel's real name. *Don't call him Angel,* I remind myself. *That would be like, peak weird.*

Tag. It fits him. Big, hunky, strong and silent. I wonder what it's short for. Taggart? Is it some obscure Celtic name?

"Tag," I repeat, handing a bill to Murph to cover the drinks and turning to him. "Now we're on equal footing, at least."

"Oh, shit. I didn't introduce myself." Tag lights up with a sheepish grin that makes me relax instantly. "I'm such an ass. Or Tag. Whichever you prefer."

"I'll forgive you, Tag," I wink. "You've earned a few freebies."

Tag just quirks a brow, holding my gaze. And then it hits me what I just said, and a blush swamps me. I squeak softly, and he breaks into a laugh.

"Thank you for my drink," Tag tells me. "What should we toast to?"

I hastily lower my mojito and pretend I wasn't about to swallow it all in one gulp to take the edge off my nerves. "Uh… new beginnings."

"Yes," Tag hums, gazing away for a moment. Then he looks at me again and holds up his glass of wine. "Perfect. To new beginnings."

I clink my glass against his, trying not to spill any mojito into his wine, and finally take a sip. If he notices my hands trembling, he very kindly doesn't say anything about it.

"You want to sit at the front and listen?" I ask, my gaze nervously roaming over our seating options.

Tag just smiles at me. "I'm not interested in hearing anyone else tonight." He leads me over to a table against the back wall instead.

Oh, my God, I'm melting into a live and unfiltered puddle.

It's happening. It's really happening!

CALEB

I've always wanted a man who doesn't play games or beat around the bush, but now that I've found one, I hardly know what to do.

I fan myself with a hand and give a playful giggle, but Tag doesn't seem to expect a response. He guides me into a chair, and even tucks my chair in against the table before sitting down.

Is this guy straight out of Hollywood, sent to capture my heart? I kind of want to squeal and grab my phone and call everyone I know while this moment lasts.

Unfortunately, nobody I know is here. That's my own fault. I didn't invite anyone, because I was scared to death that it'd all go wrong.

And I was right to worry. It almost did, if not for Angel—Tag, I mean.

"Thank you for the help." I have to say that first—but I'm dying to know *why* he did it.

Tag just blinks, like he's already forgotten what he did. "Oh. No sweat. I own a business, so I'm always pitching," he says with a casual shrug. "I know what it's like to go into a room cold."

I tilt my head. "Pitching what?"

"Yeast, on the good days," Tag says with a grin that invites me to share a joke I don't quite get. I smile through my confusion, and he hastily adds, "Oh. I make mead."

Mead? Or meat? Like, sausages? I'm pretty sure he said mead… I tilt my head.

Before I can say a word, he adds, "Honey wine."

"Oh!" I look behind the bar and back to him. "I've seen it on the menu around town." Oh, God. I don't want to offend him by admitting I've never tried it. I usually stick to my tried and true. If breath mints could make you tipsy, that's a mojito. Ideal.

But Tag just offers me an easygoing grin. "Yeah, that's mine," he says like it's no big deal. "How about you? Are you a roving poet with a lute?"

I almost choke on my mojito at the mental image. I played a lot of video games as a teen—nerd, remember—and now all I can see is myself as a quirky NPC standing in a town square with a lute.

"No. I'm an accountant," I admit, rubbing my shoulder with my arm tightly pressed against my chest. I want to hug myself to calm down every part of me that's so excited I just know I'll screw it up.

"Oh," Tag says with a light smile. "Poetry and numbers. They don't usually go together, do they?"

I shrug. "I think they do. It's hard to explain, but…" I set down the mojito as I struggle for words, my fingertips running along the glass. "The part of my brain that likes everything to be in tidy rows and columns, every problem to have a source… just loves poetry. It's the same thing, just with words."

Tag nods and leans back in his chair, his legs sprawled open in a casual, confident stance that I envy. I'm all tucked in on myself, trying not to fidget out of my skin.

This feels like a blind date. And I… kind of love it.

I've never *actually* been on a date. Not an official one, where we called it a date and talked about our families and tried to imagine fitting into each other's lives.

I've "met up for coffee" with a few guys and flirted with others right here at this bar, but it always fizzles out when I tell them I'm looking for more than one night. Being on dating apps made me feel like shit, so I deleted them. And most of the eligible men around town seem to have boyfriends already.

But Tag is interested. Even a totally clueless dork like me can tell.

"So, what brought you to town?" I ask, tilting my head as I fidget with the straw in my tall, slender glass. "I don't think you're local, are you?"

His accent is hard to place, neutral but with an East Coast twang.

Tag smiles and buries his nose in his wine glass, his gaze lifting like he's thinking. At last, he lowers his glass and shrugs. "I visited and didn't want to leave. I realized I wanted to get away from it all. The stress, the people, the constant *busy*ness."

Now I'm all tingly. I'll never get tired of hearing people fall in love with my hometown. "Yeah," I agree with a nod. "This place is great for that. Lots of big city types end up here. Especially when they want to settle down, start families, all that stuff."

I'm totally fishing here. Guys who just want to get laid will panic and run a mile when I say that.

Tag just smiles and shrugs. "I might start a family one day. Just need the right guy first. What about you? Did you grow up here?"

"Born and raised," I say with a proud smile. "I never had my *gotta get out to the big city* phase. I guess I'm lucky. It's so gay-friendly here, and my family was supportive, too. I didn't have anything to run away from, or to go discover. Nothing I couldn't find here."

Except what it's like to actually be with men instead of gazing at them from across the room. But I am *not* telling him that I'm a twenty-something virgin. I need at least one more mojito first.

Okay, half a mojito. I'm a lightweight. Sue me.

Tag raises his glass to toast that. "I'm glad," he says. "My family's back home in Maryland, but they supported me from the start, too. I've always felt lucky."

I nod my agreement. I've got a few gay friends, and not all of them have been so fortunate. "Even if my brothers are assholes sometimes. But that's siblings, huh?" I grin.

"I'm the only kid," Tag admits and chuckles. "Good for scoring leftovers at Thanksgiving, though. Do you have a big family?" Tag tilts his head and settles back.

"Three older brothers. A biochemist, a pediatrician, and a family lawyer. I'm the numbers nerd—and the baby of the family."

Tag beams at me. "Aww. Wow. Those are big footprints to follow. The accountant thing makes sense."

I open my mouth for a moment to brush it off, and then close it. He just understood—without my saying a word—that a creative career was off the table from the very start.

His perceptiveness catches me off-guard. He's right. All three of them are super-talented in respectable careers in science, medicine, and law. Poetry? Not so much.

"Yeah, they are." I shrug. "Maybe one day I could leave behind the spreadsheets and just be a poet. But I don't think many people get to do that, you know?"

First, I need to get good at it—and learn how to read them out loud without dying of embarrassment. I confronted my biggest fear today.

Their slightly too polite applause is still squirming around in my gut, tormenting me with self-doubt. Is that reaction any better than being laughed off the stage? I'd rather know where I stand than have to guess.

Apart from my family, most people don't even know I *write* poems, much less that I dream of doing it full-time. It's my own dirty little secret. Well, one of them. But I'm still half a mojito away from spilling the rest.

"You never know," Tag tells me, his voice gentle but sincere. "I really enjoyed that first one. What was it about?"

Oh, crap. I open my mouth as my cheeks flush. *The fact I'm a big gay virgin? No, think of something more eloquent than that!* "Uh..."

I clear my throat and stir the straw around, frantically hoping for some ice cubes to melt so I can sip my drink and buy myself more seconds. But Tag just waits patiently, unhurried and not even fazed by how easily I get flustered.

When my throat unclenches, words return to my brain, and I let them flow. "Longing. When you want something so badly, but it seems so far out of reach."

Tag leans forward and nods, setting his empty wine glass down. "I felt that," he agrees. His voice is soft and intimate all of a sudden. "There was a fragility, too. It was bittersweet. Like when you really like someone and you want to see more of them, but you can't quite bring yourself to ask."

Tag's eyes pin me to the spot as he picks through my deepest desires and lays them on the table where I can't ignore them anymore.

I blush, but there's no ignoring Tag's searching gaze. He's watching me like he's seeking permission to keep flirting with me. Normally I'd shut him down right here with some lame excuse and run away.

I'm tired of hiding from what I want.

I'm terrified of asking Tag out and screwing up this insanely awesome chemistry that makes every fiber of my body quiver with pleasure. But I'll never get to the next step if I don't actually try. It's time. Way past time. Like, at least eight years past time.

Being openly gay in high school was fine. I never had to hide the lisp or keep my wrists rigidly straight to stay safe. But I wasn't the hot football star or the class president. Nobody ever took me to the movies to hold hands and awkwardly giggle.

And I sure as hell don't know how adult dating works, except for putting up some cute photos of yourself on Grindr and getting an endless stream of dick pics. Not my thing.

A date. I can do it. Just one little date.

"You want to do it?" I ask, clutching my glass in front of my chest in both hands like a shield.

Tag's brows climb, one at a time. "Whoa," he teases. "I didn't expect that."

His wicked grin makes him even *more* fucking gorgeous. My misfiring brain is way more interested in his dimples and the flash of his white teeth than actually remembering what the conversation is supposed to be about.

"Fuck. Sorry. A date!" I squeak.

My throat is tight. Screw butterflies—boulders tumble around my stomach. I want to dive under the table and hide from his amused grin. But I don't want to miss a moment of his beautiful smile, either.

Fuck. I'm crushing so hard.

"Do it like, ask me," I keep bumbling on as he grins. "I mean, I'm basically asking you to ask me. Which means I'm asking you. Oh, God. I'm *trying* to ask you out…"

"I'd be delighted," Tag tells me, finally showing mercy. He reaches across the table to touch the back of my hand.

A burst of heat flashes through my whole body, a tingling warmth that starts in my knuckles and radiates up my arms into my brain, down into my very tippy-toes. He keeps his hand there, so I clumsily set down my glass. My fingertips are icy-cold, but I turn my hand over.

Tag rests his fingers in my palm, and I close my hand around his, relishing the sudden heat. Is it my imagination, or is the whole world spinning around me? I can hardly breathe.

This is what I've been missing? Holy crap.

"C-Cool. Like, tomorrow?" I ask like I've said it a million times before. I'm not sure how I'll survive twenty-four hours without spending every minute staring into space and giggling.

"Tomorrow's perfect." Then Tag bites his lip and frowns. "My evening's pretty busy. I have a new batch that needs racking. Do you have a lunch hour? We could meet for coffee."

I have no idea what that first part means, but that's only *sixteen* hours to wait, which is one-third less torment. Even fewer if you ignore the hours asleep. Or trying to sleep. "Yeah, great." I hope I sound somewhat cool. "How about noon at The Purple Cellar?"

Is it too fancy? Especially for lunch? I just want it crystal-clear that this is a *date*, not a friend-date.

"Perfect." Tag's got the message. He squeezes my fingers gently and lets go of my hand, leaning back. "I'm driving, so I can't drink any more," he says with an apologetic smile. "And I've got some work stuff to finish up tonight." Before the crashing disappointment can swamp me, he digs out his phone. "Let's swap numbers, just in case?"

I nod eagerly and take his phone, entering my name and number. When he hands me back my phone, I notice that he's entered *Tag* as his name followed by a bee emoji.

"Hold on. If we're going to be fancy..." I snatch back his phone before he can take it and edit my name field to add the symbol of an open book. "There."

"Perfect. I'll text once I get home," Tag says with a grin when I finally let him have his phone back. He rises to his feet, and so do I.

Crap. I don't know if I should hug him goodbye, or blow a kiss, or wave, or... I freeze on the spot, hands outstretched like Cristo Redentor, that huge statue over Rio de Janeiro. Smooth. Real smooth.

Tag breaks through the fog of indecision and steps closer to wrap his arms around me in a warm but brief hug.

If one touch of my hand was enough to scorch me, this is like embracing a forest fire. But I fling my arms around his neck for these too-brief moments as my whole body crackles and sings.

When he pulls away, I'm suddenly way more dizzy than I was before, and the room seems to float around me.

"Great meeting you, Caleb," Tag tells me and runs his hand back through his hair like he's completely unaware that he's leaving me with the sexiest parting image of the night. "See you at noon."

"Tomorrow," is my super-smooth parting greeting. Not *thanks again,* or *can't wait,* or *have a good night.* But before I can make my mouth come up with better words, he's gone, and the whole room seems a little darker.

Suddenly I'm not interested in staying for one more moment. I need to be alone so I can squeal and dance around and enjoy the high that's vibrating through me. I'm not going to get a wink of sleep, but suddenly, I don't mind.

Not one bit.

4

TAG

"Not that one. Not that one. Not that one…"

Scowling, I shove the hangers to the side one at a time like they've mortally offended me. I have a couple of plain black and white shirts for tastings and business meetings. But I don't want my look to say *business partner*. I want to be *hot yet enigmatic first date*.

My row of plaid shirts stretches on, making it more likely I roll with *weirdo lumberjack who lives in the woods*.

I've gotten spoiled by living in Burlington, where nobody cares what you wear as long as you're legal. They're even relaxed about that, probably banking on short summers keeping the nudists indoors.

I've never been a clothes horse. I'm good to go in a T-shirt and jeans. I used to rely on our band's manager to approve or veto outfits for photo shoots and interviews. But goddamn, I want to make a good impression on this guy.

Caleb is an adorable, shy little nerd and I'm already falling for him hook, line, and sinker. No point in denying it. If I weren't, I could have just made excuses and left last night. But I let him keep me for a drink and a chat and even agreed to go have lunch today.

But I've been avoiding the whole dating thing for years. Relationships of all kinds, if I'm really honest. Now I have no clue what to wear, say, or do.

We got some of the awkward first-date questions out of the way last night, but those are important conversational fallbacks. What if we just sit in silence?

Worse still, what if I tell him too much? I want him to get to know the real me, not Google my Wikipedia page the second I get up for the bathroom.

No, I can't slip up. I won't. I haven't so far, and I intend to keep up that track record.

"This one," I mutter at last, grabbing a dark blue shirt that I'd like to think brings out my eyes or some shit. I've gotten compliments on it, so it must work for me.

I've already showered, carefully trimmed my beard close to my jawline, and styled my hair. Also, I've brushed my teeth three times. Not because I'm a peppermint fetishist or clean-teeth freak, but purely accidentally. I've spent all morning daydreaming about Caleb's starry eyes and golden curls and I keep forgetting what I'm doing.

Lunchtime snuck up on me awfully fast after spending twice as long to measure specific gravity as it usually takes, thanks to my mental images of a smiling Caleb.

I've really gotta get my ass in gear or risk standing him up.

"Okay. Good. Wallet-keys-phone," I mumble and slap my pockets to make sure it's all in there. "Get going, Tag. That's all you need. That and a winning smile." I flash the mirror one more grin, trying to will my usual confidence to come back, wherever it's hiding.

When you've walked away from everything despite the warnings, you stop giving a shit about what other people think. But I *do* give a shit what Caleb thinks. I'm not sure what to make of this new development.

Queenie tries to persuade me to smuggle her in, but I scratch her head and promise that she'll meet him on the next date.

Whoa. Next date? Slow down there, cowboy.

I'm so caught up in thought that I hardly notice the drive to The Purple Cellar. My farmhouse is only a ten-minute drive away. Lunchtime on a Monday is about as busy as it gets, which means waiting patiently for two or three other cars to find parking before it's my turn.

After easing the truck into a spot, I jump out and lock up, then head straight for the front door in case Caleb is here early.

Is that him already? The curls identify him a mile off. And I thought I was early!

"Sorry," I greet him. "Am I late?"

Caleb lights up like a Christmas tree. He beams at me and then flings his arm around me, kissing my cheek. "No. I'm just even earlier."

He lets go and tells me how his boss is great and doesn't mind him going to lunch early, but I'm hardly listening.

My whole body is tingling with something indescribable. But good. Unfamiliar. Caleb is a magnet, and every inch of me has just pointed to him. And I do mean *every* inch.

Keep it in your pants, I warn myself, but it's a flimsy warning at best. Holy crap. I haven't felt a man's touch in months, and certainly not the romantic kind. I'd forgotten how fast and hard the wave of *feeling* swamps the brain.

I like him. I really want him to like me, too.

My whole body is still buzzing from that one warm brush of lips on my cheek. It wasn't like he French-kissed me and dipped me to the sidewalk or anything. But try telling my dick that.

Suddenly I realize there's silence and he's waiting for me to say something. Shit. I scratch the back of my neck. "I'll camp out here like it's the Apple Store next time."

Caleb laughs, a soft sound that sets my heart alight. "Shall we? Since we're both early?"

"Hope that's not a prediction of things to come," my idiot mouth says before my brain catches up. Then I catch my breath, my eyes flying wide open.

But Caleb isn't offended or judgmental. He just laughs as he turns bright red, nearly smacking himself in the face with the door. He leaps back straight against my chest.

"Whoa," I laugh, my arm going around his waist as one foot goes back to brace us both. And for a brief, perfect second it's like we're dancing together, his back nestled perfectly against my chest.

Fuck. I did *not* need to find out that he fits perfectly against me as a little spoon.

"S-Sorry!" Caleb's voice squeaks at the very end of the word. He pulls away from me and strides through the door. Damn it, my whole heart starts glowing like a firefly as I watch him trying to pretend he's not flustered.

But that does raise a few questions, and not just in my pants.

Once we're seated at the table, I run my fingers along the edges of the linen menu. "So... hi."

"Hi," Caleb says breathlessly, clutching the menu in front of his chest again like he's trying to stop me perving on him. Smart move. Left to my own devices, I might stare at the ripple of his shirt over his chest for hours.

"I'm glad we were brave yesterday," I tell him, sliding my foot forward until my toe nudges his. "Can we try it again today?"

I really, honest to God, do mean *we*. A concert in front of thousands would make me less nervous than Caleb's eyes.

"Yes," Caleb whispers, a smile rounding out those dimples. "It's a deal." He sets down the menu and nervously touches all his cutlery. He opens his mouth, but before he can say anything, the waiter arrives with a glass jar of water and a bread basket.

I send him away with our thanks, then grin. "What were you about to say?"

"I-I don't remember." Caleb stares at the bread basket like a starving man. "I forgot how good their garlic butter is. But it's garlic."

"If we're both eating it, who'll notice?"

"My whole office. I'll be garlic burping all day. Wait. Should I say that on a first date?"

I tip my head back and laugh, startled by his honesty. I love that he isn't pretending to be some perfect, airbrushed model.

"Is this a first date?" Caleb follows up and tilts his head. "Are we counting last night?"

I bite back my grin at what that sounds like. Caleb doesn't even notice the innuendo, and I'm not going to give him the wrong impression about what I'm after. Instead, I clear my throat. "I think it's the second date, so you're safe."

"I don't know how dating works at all," Caleb admits. It's not self-deprecating, though, just a statement of fact.

"That makes two of us." I reach over the table for a high-five, and before I can second-guess that decision, Caleb grins and smacks his palm delicately against mine before flapping his wrist out.

"Oof, mistake. Crow pose nearly murdered my wrist this morning. No high-fives. Strictly fist bumps. Or hand-holding. That works too."

I grin at him. "Noted."

I love the way he doesn't try to be all stiff and manly and reserved. He's unapologetic about who he is. He isn't trying to act straight, or tone down his accent. He walks with a swish and talks with a lisp.

Despite his stage fright, on some level Caleb doesn't care what people think of him, and that's incredibly attractive.

After we order and the waiter leaves, I brace myself for the dreaded silence. Caleb probably doesn't want to talk about poetry all day and be reminded of the hard road he faces if he wants his dream career.

What do we talk about when my past and his future are off the table?

For a moment, guilt tries to slip into my brain and nibble away at my good mood.

No way.

If this is going somewhere, I can't keep it secret for our whole life together, but… there's a time and a place, and right now is neither.

Burlington is big enough to be virtually unknown, but small enough that my presence would become gossip. The kind people whisper about all over town—or even the country.

Caleb isn't the type who would deliberately alert the tabloids for a payoff. But he's absolutely the type to get scared off by dating a guy whose face used to be in them.

I've worked my ass off for years to build my new, anonymous, simple life. Worse than being scared off by my fame would be if Caleb were drawn to me *because* of it.

I want him to like me for me, not who I was. Better to keep my old life under wraps and see where this date leads. I'll show Caleb who I am now. The past can wait.

Thankfully, the silence is over. Caleb is filling the uncertain void of the space between us with more of his adorable, super-distracting, flustered conversation.

"So I guess I should ask what you're looking for—or start by telling you? I'll start. Is that okay?"

I grin. "Perfect," I tell him, curious about his answer. Frankly, whatever he wants… he can get.

Not only is Caleb a hot nerd, but he's talented, sincere, and unapologetic about who he is. He just needs a nudge to see that he deserves to be confident in his talent.

Caleb draws a breath and lets it out. "Cool," he murmurs with a determined nod. "So I want to find a boyfriend, not just… a hookup. But all the guys I've met only seemed to want to hook up, so I've never really dated anyone. Or been on a date. This is the first one. If it wasn't obvious from my incredibly smooth pickup lines last night."

I can't hide my surprise. I set down my water glass and sit up straight, staring at him. "This is your first date?" I repeat.

No way. Suddenly, my favorite poem of his makes more sense, but also less. He's a catch. So maybe he's been locked in a tower doing the accounts for a witch on the edge of town. It's the only explanation.

Caleb wags his finger. "Second, remember?"

"My bad." I wink at him. "So, last night was your first date?"

Caleb sighs and bites his lower lip, a cloud of worry appearing on his face. "That sounds so childish, you know? I hate telling people that."

I shake my head. "You look around my age. Twenty…"

Caleb playfully folds his arms and grins at me, challenging me to finish. Oh, crap. I've opened a Pandora's box now.

I hesitate and narrow my eyes. "Tw…thr…f…" my mouth moves in exaggerated strange shapes.

"Six," Caleb finally breaks down and finishes for me, giggling. "Twenty-six."

Phew. That's about what I'd guessed. "I'm twenty-nine."

Caleb nods. "Cool," he concludes, then picks up his water glass. "And what about you?" he asks and takes a long drink.

"Well," I murmur, staring at the table so I'm not hypnotized by the bobbing movements of his Adam's apple. "I'd like more than one-night stands. Compatibility in bed is important to me, don't get me wrong. But… I'm starting to think about the rest of my life now, you know?"

Caleb nods, his eyes lighting up. "Exactly. I'm not *not* interested in sex. I just… want romance, too."

In his soft words, I hear the same longing that I feel on lonely evenings by the fire, just stroking Queenie and staring into the distance.

"Me, too," I whisper. I might be out of the game, but even I can tell an invitation when I hear one. His hand is just lying there, right next to the bread basket, *asking* to be taken.

So I do it. I reach over the table and rest my palm over the soft back of his hand. I try to figure out how to tell him that I want to find out what makes him tick, and listen to his fears, and make him smile.

If that's romance, then yeah, I want it.

But then the waiter arrives. Damn it, universe.

We both giggle like middle-schoolers caught holding hands in the lunch room, and I let go of him so I can move my glass out of the way and make space for the plate.

But that thread between us, the spark that fires through the air whenever we look at each other… it's still there, whether or not we're touching.

That's a good start. A really good start.

As we unfold our napkins, Caleb asks how my day is going and what I have to do with the mead tonight. I'm relieved for the chance to talk about something I know, but I try to keep my answers short so I don't bore him. Not a lot of people have heard of mead, so I'm used to explaining the process.

Caleb seems fascinated, though, and then he starts to talk about his day, and the conversation grows even easier. All I have to do is listen and make sounds like I know what he's saying.

Our precious lunch hour flies by all too quickly. By the time we've finished eating, it feels like we've known each other for years. I love hearing the methodical way his brain works.

"So I've told my coworkers I'll design a new macro today to fix all of that, because *honestly*, who needs a spreadsheet to tell them how to fix their spreadsheet?" Caleb clicks his tongue.

"Uh huh." I smile goofily at him. "I just want you to know I understood about twenty percent of that, if we're being generous."

Caleb laughs. "It's okay. I don't know anything about bees or booze. Well, making booze. I know how to drink it, as long as it's sweet."

There's my chance.

"I have a tasting room in my meadery, you know. Would you like to try it?" I scratch my neck nervously. "If you'd rather stick to mojitos, I won't be offended. I might have to go get some ingredients, though…"

Caleb grins. "No, I'd love to see more of what you're passionate about."

"I only have one condition," I tell him with a playful smile so he doesn't get worried. "I share my mead, you share your poems."

He laughs. "Okay, it's a deal. Where do you live?"

"Um…" I hesitate. "Out in the woods. It's about a ten-minute drive away. I can pick you up. Full disclosure: the meadery is in my back yard. If you're more comfortable, we could figure out a nice day for a picnic…"

Caleb snorts. "I like my fingers and toes attached. Besides, aren't you supposed to go home together on the third date?"

Relief makes my heart soar, but I laugh anyway. "Those rules are bullshit. People should do what they want, when they want."

"And I want to see your meadery."

For some reason, my brain decides the best answer to that is, "And my dog wants to meet you."

But Caleb hardly misses a beat. "You have a dog? Dude. If you'd told me that, we could be at your place *right now*. Where are my doggy scratches?"

I burst out laughing as I reach over the now-cleared table to take his hand again. "I'll make up for it. When's good?"

"Tomorrow?" Caleb suggests. "Or are you still busy then?"

"Nope, tomorrow's great." I don't care how long it takes—I'll finish my work tonight so that my schedule is free for him.

Holy crap. I've never thought that about anyone since moving here. Maybe I can let myself fall for this guy.

Or maybe I don't have a choice—I'm already head over heels.

5

CALEB

"Let me get this straight." Lee folds his arms as he looks at me across the dinner table. "You read your poetry out loud, this hot guy came up and asked you out, and now you're going to his house in the deep dark woods."

"Alone," Elijah interjects from my right, helpful as always.

Lee nods. "Alone."

Oh, God. All I wanted was help choosing which poems I should bring on the date. I should have known better.

The whole family is here for dinner: my parents, all three of my brothers, and my sisters-in-law. Lily, Anna, and Sarah take pity on me and rescue me sometimes, but not tonight. They're just as curious as my brothers.

Kelvin holds up a hand, and I cross my fingers under the table, hoping he takes my side. Instead, he pipes up with exactly the words I was afraid of hearing. "You didn't tell us about the reading."

His frown is genuinely disappointed. More than the other two, he thinks my poetry is "pretty good," to quote him exactly from the last time I emailed him some of my new work.

My cheeks are hotter than the sun. I grab my glass of sparkling water while I attempt a casual shrug. "It was just open mic night, nothing fancy."

When I look at Mom, she's frowning too, the mirror image of Kelvin. "We would have come to support you. I hope you know that," she says, like every mother is obligated to tell their child.

"I know," I promise her.

"Getting back to this guy who's trying to get in Caleb's pants," Lee says. I'm not sure if I'm relieved about the subject change. His wife, Sarah, elbows him, but he ignores her. She's used to him being the shit-stirrer. "We need to know more."

"Maslow's hierarchy disagrees," I mutter.

"Boys, let him finish his supper in peace," Dad says, but he's smiling. He never takes anything seriously, and he rarely takes sides. In snowball fights and family arguments, he's Switzerland. I suppose it's a good policy when you have four boys, but I've often wished he'd make the others quit it.

I shouldn't have told my brothers about any of this. Unfortunately, my face is an open book and I'm terrible at hiding anything.

Lee grins and pushes a potato wedge around the lemon-cream sauce on his plate. "We could talk about the deck," he suggests.

I'd rather not spend the rest of supper being teased for my nerdy virgin status. But I'm the only one in favor of that idea. The women all roll their eyes at each other, including Mom.

Lee knows perfectly well that nobody wants to talk about the deck one more time.

Mom and Dad keep saying they want to replace their deck, but they're always putting it off. This summer, we decided to just put our heads together and get it done. We couldn't get past the stage where we staked it out with pencils stuck into the ground and string. They stayed out there for two months while we argued about lumber and dimensions until the birds stole the strings for their nests.

The thought of us trying to actually build the thing? I'm not sure if it would be a comedy or a tragedy. We'd end up on some Youtube DIY "you tried" channel— if we even finished.

"Not the deck," Kelvin sighs. "It's October. It's too late to build this year."

"I mean, if we're serious about it, we *should* plan for the spring," I insist in vain.

"It might be too late to build, but it's never too late for love," Eli agrees, straight-faced. The oldest of us, he's the devil's advocate. I often remind him that his knack for spotting the truth is better left in his career in family law.

Lee gives an exaggerated wink. "I don't know if *love* is what we're talking about."

"Otherwise, the warm weather will sneak up on us again."

Sometimes I wonder if anyone listens to me around here. Other times I know damn well they don't.

"Are you sure it's a date? Is he looking for an accountant?" Lee asks.

I know he's just trying to get a rise out of me because he's stung that I didn't invite them to the reading.

Still, the jab works. He's grown up enough that he rarely holds me in a headlock while poking my chest, but he's mastered the verbal equivalent.

"*Yes*, I'm sure," I tell him, irritation rising in my throat. "He didn't check my qualifications first."

"Qualifications? Is that we're calling it these days?" Eli can't resist cracking a joke, and the others laugh. Even Dad hides a smile.

"Boys," Mom interrupts, and I cast her a grateful look. "No fighting at the table. Someone get dessert. There's a lemon meringue pie."

Thank God. This is my big break. "I'll do it," I insist before anyone else has a chance.

"I'll help get the plates," Anna offers and accompanies me to the kitchen. Mercifully, she doesn't say anything, just gives me a sympathetic smile. It's an open-plan layout anyway, so I don't even have a wall to hide behind.

Anna gathers the stack of dessert plates and piles the forks on top while I get the meringue.

"Be careful, though," Kelvin tells me, leaning back in his chair to look around the others at me.

The secondborn of us all and Anna's husband, Kelvin is a pediatrician. He saves his bedside manner for his patients, but he often sees interpersonal problems where there aren't any.

Anna sets the dessert plates in front of him, and he kisses her cheek and automatically starts passing out plates and forks.

"Of what?" I ask, balancing the meringue in my hands. "I'm very coordinated. I hardly ever drop dessert."

He misses the not-so-subtle hint—or ignores it—and carries on down the same path.

"You don't know the guy at all. Just because he's a fan doesn't mean he's got good intentions."

"Let's be proud that our Caleb has fans," Mom says with a smile. I know she'd feel differently if this were my career, but they've always supported our hobbies. I'll take what I can get.

Once I put the meringue on the table, I drop heavily into my chair. "*Thank you*, Mom."

"I can ask around and see if anyone knows him. Tag, right?" Lee asks, kicking my leg when I don't look at him. "Come on, little bro. Living out in the woods by himself like a hermit. Only moved to town a few years ago. Definitely a serial killer. Does anyone know his address?"

"He bought that cute little place with the couple of acres and a garage. Eli and I looked at it," Lily says.

"The guy with the bees, right? Oh, yeah. That place. I know where it is," Eli says.

"Don't you dare try to play chaperone," I warn him with a death glare. "I'm a grown man."

I don't feel like one when my brothers pile on the teasing. I might as well be in middle school again, looking up to all my high-school big brothers.

"Sorry," Eli says, and he actually sounds serious. "But we're worried, that's all."

"Here, who's cutting the meringue?" Anna's working with me now, trying to defuse the conversation. She holds up a knife, and Dad takes it and starts cutting wedges.

I'm the overly-protected baby brother of the family. It sucks, feeling so inexperienced. They're only a couple of years older than me, but they're all married and settled down, but here I am dating for the first time.

"I'm glad you're getting out there," Kelvin says with an encouraging smile. "But people are looking for different things."

"You don't have to tell me that twice." I snort. "Why do you think I haven't found a boyfriend yet?"

"Aw, don't be so hard on yourself." Lee smirks as I flip him off. "What if he just wants to get laid?"

Maybe I'd like that, I think, but no way am I saying that in front of Mom and Dad. I've always been the prude of the family.

"Is that a bad thing?" Eli shrugs. Apparently the devil's advocate switch has flipped the other way now that he's gotten a reaction. "Do what you want, Caleb."

"Might make him loosen up a little," Lee snorts.

"*Lee,*" Sarah scolds him, and he finally sighs and nods at her.

Eli takes my side, too. He elbows Lee. "Don't talk that way about our sweet little Caleb. Let him blossom at his own pace."

"But we *are* all curious about this guy who's caught your eye," Mom tells me, which makes me want to disappear into a hole. "We're looking forward to meeting him sometime."

I get the feeling she's teasing me in her own way, but I do appreciate hearing that. My family has always been supportive of me being gay.

I think they were worried that I'd struggle more than the others to find love. It's true, but not because I'm gay. Just because I'm a giant nerd and I'm working with a smaller dating pool.

"It's only a date, not marriage," I grumble. "Don't go scaring him off now."

With that, they finally let the subject die, to my huge relief. The rest of the lemon meringue pie disappears amidst arguments about whether we can learn to build over the winter.

I barely participate, and Anna, Kelvin, and Mom all notice. They keep giving me worried glances, so I smile at them like everything is fine. Truth is, I'm way too busy inside my own head to say much.

What *is* so special about me? I mean, I don't hate myself or want to become a different person. Far from it. I'm okay with myself. I just don't think other people are really into the kind of person I am.

I've never thought of myself as the type to be pretty and interesting and captivating. Yet Tag's moving fast. Or is it me? I'm the one who asked him to The Purple Cellar.

But I have to follow my instincts, and they say not to let him go. Give it a try, even if I fall flat on my face and come off like a shy little geeky virgin.

Tag's into shy nerds. That helps a lot with the whole confidence thing. And for my part, I'm crazy about him—he has a way of listening that makes me feel… well… *seen*, not just heard.

And he seemed genuine when he said that he was looking for a boyfriend, just like me.

Wouldn't be the first time a guy said that and didn't mean it. Usually it's followed by some kind of statement like, *But in the meantime, I'll have fun until the right one comes along.*

I've always shut them down there, rather than agree to a first date full of wheedling and innuendo.

Tag didn't try any of that shit over our glass of wine. Our second date… it was different from what I expected, too. Mature and simple and absolutely thrilling.

I know him better than they think, I tell myself as I get up to gather the empty plates. *He's not a serial killer, that's for sure. And if he's a playboy, is that so bad?*

I've been so determined to find The One that I've been ignoring guys who could end up being great for me.

Chemistry might not be everything, but when he's around, I suddenly see why it matters so much. It helps lubricate conversation.

So to speak. I bite back a smile.

Maybe I should stop overthinking this. Tag is just who I need to bring me out of my shell. For once, I'll ignore my brothers stifling me with bubble-wrap and good intentions, planting worries in my head.

Good things can happen without me creating probability models of disaster.

TAG

My first mistake was not looking at the phone before I answered. In fairness, though, I'm a little distracted. My life is chaos. I'm surrounded by a chaotic mess of rubber hoses and filter parts.

"Yello?" I drawl as I turn the valve off to stop the flow of mead. The last thing I need is to get distracted and end up flooding the place before Caleb even shows up.

"Tag, hey," a familiar, light voice greets me. I freeze in place and then slowly straighten up, whipping the phone away from my ear to check.

Goddamn. I didn't expect to hear from Roxanne Richardson today. Or any other day. My former band's agent doesn't get in touch often. Just around Christmas to say hello, and I suspect to check that I'm still alive.

I don't begrudge her silence. She cares about me, but she cares about Jet Slack more. And I respect that. My band—no, *the* band, I remind myself—is still out there. They're winning awards and selling out stadiums and demanding every minute of her time.

But it's only October. Where's the fire?

"Hey," I finally manage to greet her, swallowing the trepidation. "How's life?"

Don't tell me they want me to take part in some stupid documentary. Or worse still, an interview. Roxy knows I don't do interviews anymore.

"Crazy. You know, same old same old," Roxy says with a laugh. She sounds tired, but not much is new there. I don't know how the woman is still alive—she just seems to run on coffee and fumes. "You? Have you found serenity?"

"It dwells in me every—" I trip over a hose, send an empty bucket flying with a loud clatter, and swear as I grab the nearby shelf to keep me upright. "Every day."

"You'll have to share your secrets to enlightenment," Roxy says drily, and I grin.

For just a moment, it feels like the old days. Between our management team and Roxy as the no-nonsense agent, life was fast and banter kept us moving… always moving.

But that was the problem. There was never a moment to stop and think about where we were going.

I've had all the time in the world since then, and I wouldn't trade this life for that one.

"Things going well with the business, when you aren't wrecking it?"

I laugh. "Pretty good, actually. I'm in most of the local restaurants and bars. Working on a canning line so I can hit all the shelves I want to be on, too."

She whistles under her breath. "I'll keep looking for your stuff."

"Nah, you won't. Why take up valuable tequila space?" I rib her.

"Excellent point. Have you thought about making tequila?"

"Depends how much you pay me." I grin, but underneath the banter, I'm worried. *Is* she calling to offer me a payday? They never come without strings attached.

"I can pay you in records. I'm finally ditching them all. Downsizing to a studio loft with Minnie."

I whistle under my breath, my eyes widening. The only thing

more surprising than hearing her drift away from her old collection is picturing her *not* living in the apartment she's rented for years from a batty but harmless old lady. We had some great parties there.

"No shit. Are you guys…?"

"Yeah, she proposed to me last month and I said yes."

"Fuck, yes," I grin and punch the air. "I mean, congrats."

A lot of water has gone under the bridge between us, but I can still be happy for her. Roxy's a rare good person in a machine that can often grind the goodness out of people. So is Minnie, her fiancée, who manages some fancy gardens in upstate New York.

"Thanks. You're obviously invited to the wedding, but God knows when it'll be," Roxy says with a groan. "Minnie's flying to England to do some gardening show and the Chelsea show and lots of other stuff I don't understand."

"It'll be worth the wait," I promise, even if I have no clue. It's not like I've been married before. It just seems like the kind of thing you're supposed to say.

And speaking of waiting, Roxy finally gets to the reason for her call. "So, this TV producer wants to license some of the old stuff. We've negotiated a deal to make him take several and use one in another show he executive produces."

"Oh, hell yeah. Do it. Get that money," I tell her with a shrug to myself as I pop open the lid of the fermenter to check on the progress.

All the material I poured blood, sweat, and tears into… they're just history for me now. Part of my old life. I'm done with them. If I can get another payday, so much the better.

"The band members all agreed on the deal," Roxy says, her words unusually delicate all of a sudden, "so expect your share of the royalties."

Ouch. It's a sucker punch to the gut, remembering that I have no say on that stuff anymore. It was all part of the contract. I sold out and walked away. I get a slice of the royalties, but not a vote.

This is just a heads-up courtesy call, not asking permission.

"Right," I manage a moment later, forcing some cheer into my voice. "I'll choose 'highest price first' when I replace the fridge next month. Maybe it'll text me when I'm out of milk and give me backrubs."

Roxy hastily takes the escape route I offer, so neither of us have to dwell on the fact that I'm a has-been shadow from the band's youth. "I think you need a boyfriend for that."

"Damn," I groan. "The salesman really was talking out of his ass then."

I know what Roxy's really asking. I wish I had better news. Maybe if she'd called in a few days from now…

Now, don't get ahead of yourself there, pal.

Roxy laughs. "Oh, the glamorous life of home ownership. Can't wait. Fixing my own sink, can you picture it? Mrs. C's already made me swear to visit for lunch every month."

"Mmm. Good. Get those free lunches," I grunt, crouching by the fermenter and turning the tap on again. I still have a few minutes where I can divide my attention, and the day isn't getting any younger.

It's not like she needs a free lunch anymore—Jet Slack must be paying for that new condo in cash—but there's no cooking like her landlady's.

"Oh, and there's another thing," Roxy says casually. "This young guy came up and asked if I'm still representing you. Word has it he's a newbie trying to hustle up business, looking for a quick cash cow."

I snort with laughter. Crouched on tiptoe like I am, I nearly fall over. "I'm like, the opposite of what he's looking for." I told everyone pretty clearly when I left that that was it.

They didn't believe me at first, but four years of total silence has persuaded them.

"I told him that." Roxy laughs. "Oh, to be twenty and dumb again."

"No way. I'll take going-on-thirty and… well, still dumb." It was glamorous and exciting and made me feel like I was important, but then I saw the walls closing in around me.

At least I'm *me* now. I'm here, in the wide open free air.

"Yeah," Roxy murmurs, then clears her throat. The nostalgia fades as she tells me, "Right, I've got a bunch of calls to make. Look after yourself, hey?"

"You too." I smile and straighten up, fiddling with the hose to make sure it's still fed by liquid and hasn't run dry yet. "Tell Minnie I said hi—and good catch."

Roxy laughs. "Will do. See you later."

When I hang up and pocket my phone, I have a lot to think about. The minutes slide by until I'm done racking. All the clear, good stuff in the fermenter goes into one tub, and all the cloudy remnants into another.

Over time, as things settle, it'll all become clear.

I can't help myself. Once the product is all safe and sound, I scrub my hands and then head to the tasting room.

It's decorated, unlike the spartan brewing area. Accidents out there are frequent and sticky, but in here it's warm and cozy. I've got long, plush benches and little dark wood tables, a bar top made from reclaimed wood… and up on one wall, a guitar.

Not my best or most expensive. Nothing that would stand out and look too professional. But it's my favorite, an old Cort I bought in Europe on our first international tour.

Before I know it, she settles into my hands like a dream.

I strum a chord, and then another. I close my eyes and let the melody out. It's from Found Love, our first solo. It's a sharp pop rock song, but in my hands, it's almost a ballad.

My chest is full and my palms are warm with something I haven't felt in a long time. Then I stop myself and shake my head, the last note fading into thin air.

What am I doing? Caleb will be coming over in just a few hours, and I haven't even showered yet. I have a whole floor to mop, yards of stainless steel to polish. The meadery has to be spotless for this date.

For the first time in a long time, my heart wants something that money can't buy. Some*one*. Caleb—and then I picture the little open book emoji he added next to his name in my phone book, and I smile.

Yeah. I want him.

CALEB

If anyone's Cinderella in this picture, I think it's me. I snuck out at lunch today to get my hair trimmed, ironed my nicest white shirt and black trousers, and I've been drowning my lips in Vaseline.

You know, just in case.

I haven't put this much effort into my appearance since high school prom. But my big night at the ball is going to be pretty unconventional. For a start, the carriage is a white pickup truck, and as far as I can tell, the ball is happening in my date's garage.

It doesn't matter to me. The most important thing is who I'm sharing the night with, and he grins as he pulls up outside my apartment. I'm already waiting on the sidewalk, wrapped up warm in a puffy jacket and gray stretchy gloves.

Because he's literally the perfect man, Tag makes a move like he's about to climb out to open the door for me. But I'm too excited to wait for him. I shake my head and rest my foot on the truck step, hauling open the cab door and flinging myself inside.

"Hi—" I start, but before I can even get into the truck, I'm met with a warm tongue and furry chest. And I'm not talking about Tag. Someone's already in my seat, furiously wagging her tail. That someone has a loud bark, and she's not afraid to use it.

"Oh!" I squeak and nearly fall backward off the step as Queenie lunges at my face to lick me, whining with excitement.

Tag lunges toward me, but the seatbelt clicks tight and he stops short. Still, his hand is just close enough that when I flail for his hand, he grabs on tight and hangs onto me.

His strong fingers don't even slip for a moment. With him supporting my weight, I finally grab the edge of the door. My heart is racing a mile a minute, and I lose myself in a breathless giggling fit as the adrenaline hits.

"Queenie, no! Down, girl. Floor," Tag orders her.

The gorgeous chocolate Labrador doesn't want to listen. Her ears go back as she whines in protest.

"I mean it. Floor."

She reluctantly skulks into the footwell, still furiously wagging her tail as she grins up at me.

I snort with laughter. "This is your dog? You're right. She *really* wanted to meet me."

"My dog? Nah, I just borrowed her for the night so I'd look like a well-rounded guy." Tag's eyes sparkle mischievously.

"Shut up," I giggle, then realize I'm still holding his hand. And I really like it, but there are significantly less awkward ways to do it than perching on the truck step wrenching his arm out of the socket. Also, I'm sure it would be even better without gloves. "I mean, h-hi."

I finally let go of him and wipe my face with the side of my arm. I was hoping to be kissable for this man, not his Labrador.

Tag's face is flushing crimson. It's adorable, watching the red flush from his beard straight to the tips of his ears. "Hi. I'm so sorry. I should have left her at home."

"No," I laugh as the rush fades. I finally close the door after myself and reach for the seatbelt. "It's okay. Better to get the most important meeting out of the way."

Once I'm buckled in, I lean over to scratch Queenie's head. She's a chocolate Labrador with soulful brown eyes. Her tail solidly thumps the floor, and she licks my wrist, wriggling like she wants to get into my lap.

"I think that's a *yes* from her."

"I'd say." Tag's teeth flash in a grin. "That's the first boyfriend requirement met."

Boyfriend requirement? My pulse flutters in my throat. He's thinking long-term, too. It takes all I have not to squeal out loud. Instead, I purse my lips and arch my eyebrows playfully.

"Is that so? Is there going to be a test you haven't told me about?"

"I-I mean…" Tag trips over his tongue as he releases the parking brake and checks over his shoulder. "Uh, no, there's not a test."

"What are the other requirements?" I tease him, but apart from flirting, I'm genuinely curious.

His eyes flick sideways to me as he takes a moment to compose himself, then pulls into traffic. "I don't have a list, but if I did, you'd meet it."

Damn, my mysterious man is keeping his cards close to his chest. But it's okay, because his voice is a rumble that does things in my pants. *Great* things.

"Good." I grin, hoping I don't sound as blissed-out as I feel.

I'm a giggly mess the moment Tag turns his deep eyes to me. Like I'm drunk all of a sudden, before I've even had a sip. My hands are all tingly, and my head is floating in a cloud, or maybe another universe. It's intoxicating just sharing space with Tag, finally alone.

Nearly alone, as a nose pressing into my knee and wide, adoring brown eyes remind me.

"How old is she?"

"About nine months," Tag tells me. "Every time I think she's done growing, she's even bigger. But she still thinks she's a lap dog."

Hearing the affection in his voice just makes my heart flutter like a newly-emerged butterfly. It's a relief to find out how much of a dog person he is. Animals don't have any motivation to lie about who a person is, and Queenie trusts Tag.

Despite all my brothers' worrying, my instincts aren't bad. It's only experience I'm lacking... and somehow, I don't think I'll be lacking it for very long.

I've found a catch and I plan to hang onto him.

When we pull down his driveway, I can't help staring around. There are so many pretty old farmhouses around Burlington, and Tag's place is no exception.

The first building on the left looks like a barn. It's painted a cheerful, yet traditional dark red. A sign hangs above the door that reads *Silver Crown Meadery*, with a logo I'm sure I've seen before.

On the right stands a yellow farmhouse with a brick chimney, dark roof, and blue-edged windows and white shutters. The front porch is screened in with white trellis, and garden beds underneath hint at plants that grow over the top in the summer.

Attached to the side of the house is a small white garage, which is where the driveway leads. Tag presses a button attached to the sun visor, and the door rolls up.

All three buildings are set among trees that are flush with the last of the red, orange, and yellow maple leaves that mark the turning season. Winter is close. I can just picture the postcard scene when the snow settles on the huge lawn that surrounds the farmhouse to every side.

This is cozy. It couldn't be more different from my little rented apartment in the city, but just ten minutes' drive away. How crazy is that?

Queenie puts her paws on the door handle so she can see out the window, wriggling around with excitement. She obviously knows we're home. Her tail thumps my leg insistently.

"She'll run around a bit when we let her out," Tag warns me and grins. "Don't worry. It's fenced in, and she loves supper too much to run far."

"Thanks for the heads up," I laugh. Sure enough, when we

pull into the garage and Tag switches off the truck, I open the door and Queenie flies out at airplane velocity.

I laugh, twisting in my seat as I unbuckle. She's prancing around the driveway, barking and sniffing here and there. "What a character."

"She is," Tag murmurs fondly. He opens his own truck door and smiles, all his attention on me. "So, shall we?"

Suddenly, the excited nerves return. I spent most of today lost in this feeling, but it vanished with a sweet overgrown puppy begging for scratches. Now it's back—and full force.

I swallow hard and jerk my head in a nod. "Yes," I whisper. "Let's."

Tag leads the way out of the garage, hitting the button to close it after us. We head for the meadery as I steal a moment to look around. Despite the chill in the air and the evening darkness closing in, the property looks so big and private.

"It's gorgeous," I tell him. "I love this place."

Tag smiles. "Thanks. I bought the farmhouse and barn about four years ago when I moved. Fixed it up a little bit myself before admitting I didn't know what I was doing." He flashes an open grin. "Took another year to get people in to renovate everything. But it's worth the work."

"Yeah," I murmur, and I find myself brushing against his shoulder as we come to a halt in front of the meadery door. I try to pull away hastily, but Tag takes my hand in his as he fumbles with his keys to flip the right one to the top.

His big hand around mine makes my heart squeeze tight with excitement. It's a quiet promise, but I don't know what exactly he's promising me. Whatever it is, I'm on board.

We walk into the tasting room. It's elegant and cozy, with dark wood all around the room, plush purple velvet seats on the benches, and a gorgeous bar top. The light fixtures are gold and glass spirals, and on one wall hangs a beat-up old guitar.

If this were a classy little bar downtown, I'd come here every night. How didn't I hear about this before?

Before Tag closes the door, Queenie slips inside and finds a spot on the floor to curl up and put her chin on her paws.

"Wow," I murmur. "This is amazing."

"Thanks. Again, hah." Tag pulls away from me and heads behind the bar, lifting bottles onto the bar top. His eyes are alight, an excited little smile on his lips as he fetches glasses, too. "We'll just try a few things. I'm sure accounting with a hangover isn't fun."

"But worth it," I grin. "Where should I sit?"

"Wherever you like. You're the guest."

I choose a table for two with high, wooden stools upholstered in that same plush purple. Then Tag carries over a bottle and a few glasses. "If you hate it, you don't have to pretend. I won't be offended."

"I'm sure I'll love it," I promise, rummaging in my pocket for the carefully folded squares of printed poetry, unfolding and laying them flat on the table. "Same goes for my poems."

"Ah, but I've tried them before," Tag tells me with another sparkling, heart-melting grin. "I already know they're to my taste."

Then he sits across from me, so close that the insides of his knees brush the outsides of mine. I'm not quite done marveling over how so many sparks can rush through my body at once when he holds up a glass.

"To new beginnings."

"T-To beginnings," I whisper and sip the amber-colored liquid.

I expect something super-sweet, but I blink with surprise as a crisp, yet fruity taste washes across my palate. I can taste the layers of flavor like a good local honey, but not the sugar.

"Wow," I whisper. It's just as well that I don't even have to pretend to love it. "That's amazing."

Tag beams at me. "That's what I like to hear. Now, choose a poem that goes with it and hit me."

Okay, tonight is going to be awesome.

CALEB

I love tonight *so much.*

Okay, I'm probably a little tipsy. Tag has been pouring only a bit at a time, but he's given me a dozen different drinks, and I've loved almost all of them.

The one that made me wrinkle my nose was the hopped mead. It wasn't bitter like beer, but still, the fruit ones are better. True to his word, Tag wasn't offended at my reaction. He just laughed and told me that it's a love-it-or-hate-it sort of thing.

And every time I read out a poem, Tag gazes at me like he did that night we met. It seems like nothing else in the world exists when he fixes me with that stare.

The world isn't quite spinning around me—I don't want to let myself get to the point where I might not remember every single glorious detail about this date. But I'm pleasantly buzzing, my laughter coming freely at all of Tag's teasing and flirting.

It seems like we talk about anything and everything, the conversation flowing as freely as his mead. I'm happy to share my fears and hopes and dreams, and he takes everything I say perfectly seriously.

Hours must have flown past already. I can't remember the last time I enjoyed myself this much. Eventually, I feel like the end of the night must be approaching. I don't want to check the time, but I'm growing tired.

So before I lose my nerve, I wait for a lull in our conversation and finally bring up what's been on my mind all night.

"You said I'm boyfriend material. Are you looking for... another queen in your life?"

I giggle at my own pun. He's been telling me about the queen bees in his bee hives, and Queenie is still lying right there.

Tag laughs richly and strokes his finger down the back of my hand. In fact, if my head *is* spinning, I think it's his touch that's doing it. All the blood in my body seems to heat up an extra degree when he does this.

It's very distracting when I'm trying to flirt.

"Yeah. I think so," Tag murmurs, not looking away from me. "What about you?"

I nod jerkily. "I do. I've just struck out a lot," I admit softly. "Everyone seems to want to start in bed and *then* see if they're attracted to me in more of a... boyfriend sense."

Tag snorts. "I don't need to hop in bed to figure *that* out," he tells me without hesitation.

I blush and try not to die of happiness on the spot. "Yeah?"

"Yeah." Tag hesitates like he wants to say something, then sets down his glass and takes my hand in both of his. His big eyes are serious. "I really like you. I want to keep getting to know you. And if we're both happy after a few more dates... if that's what you want?"

"Then I'd let you ask me out," I tell him and bat my lashes.

Tag laughs again, the sound beautiful and rich. His voice just captivates me. Everything about him does, really.

I've never fallen for someone like this before. I don't know if this is how love is supposed to start—doesn't it take longer? Shouldn't I know everything about him first?

My heart isn't listening to any rules. I'm just charging in heart-first and head-last.

"Can I kiss you?"

Oh my God, finally! "Um, *duh*," I whisper, staring at Tag. Then I blush. Is that too forward? Maybe a little. But nobody could accuse me of hiding my true feelings.

Tag laughs and scoots his stool around the side of the table, his big arm sliding around my shoulders. I lean into him, resting one hand on his knee and the other on the low back of his stool.

My heart pounds against my rib cage as anticipation floods my body. I'm hot all over, and I can't deny that I'm already swelling to life down south. Arousal sweeps away every stray worry until all that's left is anticipation.

Tag's lips are just inches away, his big, warm body so close. I feel at home against him, so I cuddle up and smile, turning my face up towards his.

"Hi," Tag whispers. His free hand rises between us, and the back of his warm knuckles brush along my jaw.

I'm spellbound, just waiting on his move. "Hi," I manage, my voice tiny.

Tag's palm flattens on the curve of my cheek, his fingertips brushing the sensitive skin just in front of my ear. Then he leans down, all at once, and all thought disappears.

He's kissing me, his warm lips sliding and seeking. I close my eyes and let him take anything he wants. I part my lips, gasping as sparks shiver through my sensitive, smooth lips. I don't expect the bumps of his nose against mine, or the tickle of his beard, but it feels so right.

Yes. Yes, this is amazing.

"Mmm," I sigh with happiness and slide my hand around his lower back until I'm holding him, too.

This first kiss is gentle and slow, but I don't want it to end. I can hardly breathe. I need more—I need him in ways I've never allowed myself to open up to anyone.

Tag finally pulls back, the tip of his nose just brushing mine. My lips are tingling and sensitive still, and my head is *definitely* spinning. Good thing I'm still tucked in the crook of his arm.

I finally manage to let my eyes flutter open, smiling giddily up at him.

"Good?" Tag whispers.

I giggle, because I don't know what to say. "Um... *duh*," I echo myself from just moments ago. But this time I'm satisfied, glowing with happiness.

Tag grins. "Agreed." He gently pulls away, but he keeps his arm where it is, and I lean into him with a contented hum. It's awkward trying to keep my balance, and I can't stop imagining how nice this would feel on a couch.

"Glad I didn't listen to my brothers," I murmur.

"Mm?" Tag raises an eyebrow.

I raise my hand to cover my face. "I probably shouldn't say this, but my brothers thought you might be a crazy woodsman. You know, some serial killer who's going to... feed me to your bees." I grin and bite my tongue, waiting to see his reaction.

Tag's brows pull together as he gives me a dismayed stare, like he can't decide whether to say what he's thinking. "Bees don't... eat people," he finally says, his voice strained.

I burst out laughing. "That's the wrong detail to correct," I tell him. "Your face, though."

"Oh, you." Tag flicks my chest and I swat his hand away with another laugh.

"I'm not a fighter. I'm a lover. And I love sweet things." Tag gazes steadily at me, his eyes flickering to my lips and back to my eyes.

I tilt my face up and lean in, boldly pressing a brief kiss to his lips. It makes me tingle when I hear the way his breath catches in a quiet growl, like he's barely holding himself back.

When I pull away and manage to catch my breath, I steady myself once more. "So you're a serial lover? Playboy?"

Damn it, I hope my brothers *weren't* right. But no way. If he just wanted me in bed, he could have skipped the last few hours of conversation and propositioned me.

I might have even said yes, too. He *is* impossibly hot.

"Wait. No," Tag groans. "That's the wrong impression. Trust me: there's not a lineup out the door."

I snort with amusement. "Really?" He acts way more experienced than me. "You don't get out much, either?"

Tag hums and fidgets with my curls, which makes me want to purr like a kitten under his touch. His eyes are distant. I want to touch him and make him forget whatever memory he's lost in. "I used to sleep around a lot, don't get me wrong. But then I just had enough. I came here to settle down on my own. Or… I thought it would be on my own. But I guess I'm lonely."

"Me too," I murmur. "I've just been holding back for so long. Waiting for exactly the right man. Afraid of making a mistake and letting the wrong guy in."

Tag nods slightly. "Well, in my experience, we learn the most from our mistakes. But for the record, that kiss *definitely* wasn't a mistake."

I grin. "No, I don't think it was. I meant it."

"Me too." Tag runs his finger gently along my jaw. "And I don't think another date would be a mistake either."

Yes! I could almost faint off my barstool. "Let's prove it ASAP, please. Like, tomorrow? Is that too fast? Because I'd say breakfast date if I didn't have work."

Tag laughs, the sound breathy and affectionate. "Agreed," he chuckles. "Tomorrow night is too far away, but we'll make it somehow."

"By texting each other all day?"

"Deal," Tag whispers and kisses me again. This kiss lasts so long that I think I see stars bursting in front of my eyes.

When he finally pulls away, he calls the taxi for me, and it takes me about a minute to remember how to speak out loud.

"Thank you for tonight," I finally murmur. "I really enjoyed it."

"Me too." Tag helps me to my feet and even holds my jacket to help me get dressed up. "We'll text tomorrow and decide what we want to do, huh?"

"Perfect."

Tag leads me out of the meadery while Queenie stays close by our feet, sitting alongside us to wait until the taxi arrives.

"Here you are," Tag murmurs. He opens the door for me, then leans in to kiss me once more—this time just a brief hint of what tomorrow might hold. "Good night, Caleb."

"Good night, Tag." I lean down to scratch Queenie. "And to the most important girl, of course."

Queenie whines happily at me, and then trots away as Tag closes the door.

I smile all the way home, clutching my phone with both hands.

Ten minutes later, just as I stumble through the door of my apartment, there's the text.

Tag: *Let me know when you're home safe. xxx*

I grin and briefly forget I have to take my gloves off to reply, jabbing at the screen and cursing it. "Oh. Right." I toss my gloves and coat into a heap on the floor, kick off my shoes, and twirl my way to bed before collapsing on it, clutching the phone to my chest.

I've had the best night of my life, and I have the feeling it's only going to get better from here.

Thank you, fairy godmother, wherever you are.

Me: *Home and happy. xox*

Tag: *Me too. Good night, Caleb.*

Me: *Good night,*

I respond and press the phone against my chest, closing my

eyes to bask in the gooey warm happiness that floods me from head to toe.

Then I shuck my clothing in a few heartbeats and slip into bed. I can't resist poking my phone to wake it up and stare at the messages one more time before sleep takes me.

It's too early in the season for much to go wrong.

After four years of keeping bees, I can lift a hive and instantly tell how it's getting along this winter. As I check on the group of hives tucked in beneath the trees at the bottom of my property, nothing really raises my attention.

Which is just as well, because I don't have much attention to spare.

All I can seem to do today is think about the date and daydream about how perfect we are together.

Caleb was absolutely adorable last night. Everything about him captivated me, from chattering about his least favorite class in high school to telling me all about his parents' deck project.

His family sounds big, fun, and a little overwhelming. I've never met a boyfriend's parents before—when I was on the road, my relationships never lasted long. This is a whole different ball game. But I'm not going to overthink it yet.

Caleb seemed to genuinely really enjoy himself, and I'm so glad. I just want to see him as happy and confident in every area of his life.

My pocket vibrates again and I mumble a curse under my breath. I think it's Caleb, but I don't dare unzip my coat to find out. I'm not in a full bee suit, and I'm not even wearing gloves right now because the bees in the hive are all in hibernation.

I'm almost done here, so I just awkwardly heft one last hive and set it down again, breathing out heavily from the exertion. Good. Lots of honey left there. All the girls should be fine until my next check.

I stride back toward my house. Normally after a summer's day working in the hives, I might stop at the little lake at the bottom of the gentle slope. I like to sit on the stone bench and watch bees landing in their favorite mud patch for a drink.

Not in winter, though. I'm much more interested in getting inside for a hot shower.

As I make it inside, Queenie comes up for her hello scratches. "How about you warm up my hands?" I suggest. The Labrador's warm nose presses for a moment against my fingers before she high-tails it out of there. "Coward," I call after her, but she has no regrets about curling up in front of the fireplace.

I rub my hands together briskly, throw another log on the fire, and then clumsily pull out my phone.

Caleb: *Lunch break on my own today. :(I could use something sweet to liven it up.*

I grin to myself and type out a response.

Me: *I hope you don't mean me.*

Caleb: *Ha Ha. I was thinking of a drink. But if you're offering, I definitely mean you.*

My eyes widen as my grin only gets bigger. Caleb's naughty side is awakening, and I love it.

I wander toward the stairs, heading up for the top floor and my master bedroom, with its en suite and blissful hot shower. But

I barely pay attention to the stairs, busy pecking out a response as quickly as my cold fingers allow.

Me: *For you, I am absolutely offering taste testing. Name the time and place.*

Caleb: *Let's start at the Maple Factory. They have maple sugar, you know. Lots of uses for it.*

A little grunt slips from my throat as my eyes fly wide open. Oh my God, that's the last thing my sex-starved imagination needs. Now I'm going to have six boner-filled hours to contend with.

My phone goes off again.

Caleb: *Did I scare you off? ;)*

Me: *Exactly the opposite. Good thing I didn't have any more work planned today. You're very distracting.*

Caleb's message pings back straight away.

Caleb: *Taking that as a compliment.*

Me: *Oh, it is.*

Fuck. I'm already tingling from head to toe. I close my bedroom door at the top of the stairs, then toss my phone on the bed and shrug off my cold jeans and hoodie. Then the layers of shirts come off until I'm standing just in my underwear.

Caleb: *After supper at the Maple Factory for some of that sugar you're promising?*

Me: *I'll be there,*

I promise, my breath catching in my throat. As I set my phone on the bed again, I run my hands down my hips, thumbs catching my underwear to peel that last piece of clothing off.

My cock springs out, standing to attention against my stomach. I'm hard already, quivering with anticipation. I've been ignoring my own needs for a few days now, and it won't wait any longer.

"Yeah," I whisper, gazing down at the phone screen as it goes dark. Then I wrap a hand around the stiff shaft. "He plays innocent, but he knows exactly what he's doing."

And goddamn, I want him.

I keep a firm grip on my aching shaft as I walk to the marble-tiled bathroom, stepping into the spacious, glass-walled shower. I step out of the way of the water and turn the water to hot.

There's no way I'll be able to focus tonight if I don't indulge myself now. The arousal that throbs through every inch of me, straight into the pit of my belly, burns brighter at the thought.

It feels forbidden to fantasize about this man I hardly know, but in a way, that makes it more exciting. I want him *bad*.

I'll take it slowly in real life. He's a sweet little guy, and if he hasn't dated anyone… he might well be a virgin. Either way, he doesn't want to rush things, and I respect that.

But alone in the shower, I can't stop the filthy fantasies from running the show.

I groan and step sideways into the hot water, leaning back against the shower wall. The spray from the pulsating shower head caresses my body, and if I close my eyes, I can just about imagine Caleb's hot little hands running over me instead.

"Fuck," I whisper, squeezing my eyes shut. The thought of lying on my bed while he licks maple sugar from my bare skin should be silly. But instead, I'm really goddamn turned on.

I can just about feel Caleb's tongue exploring around my nipples, his hands gently running up my thighs as he sucks the sensitive nubs. Then, he'd follow up with heat of his tongue running down my stomach as my cock bounces greedily in the air.

I close my hand around myself and tug on my cock, letting my fingers tighten around the shaft all the way to the head before I slide them back to the base again.

Then I start stroking myself, a groan escaping. The rising steam floods my nostrils until my head spins, and my body is surging to life at the touch of Caleb's velvety-soft skin on my rock-hard cock.

Caleb's hand would be smaller than mine, delicate, but I can just see the wicked little smile on his lips as his innocence slips away to reveal his true desires.

"Yes," I hiss. I imagine myself looking down, seeing him naked and on his knees in front of me. His pretty lips close around the head of my cock, making heat surge through me. His other hand rises, cupping my balls and squeezing gently.

"More," I beg, the pace of my hand speeding up. "Please, Caleb. I need you."

Caleb whimpers, choking on my cock but greedily bobbing his head to take it deeper. His tongue slides around my shaft, teasing every nerve ending awake until every inch of me seems to burn.

"Fuck, fuck, fuck," I pant. The end is rushing close all too quickly. I want to let the fantasy play out for longer, but I'm on edge and desperate. "Yes, Caleb!"

My climax hits me like a freight train, blackness sparking behind my eyes as I squeeze them closed and roughly thrust into my hand. My load sprays up into the air, landing on my belly before the water washes me clean.

"Yes," I groan, long and low. My hand keeps moving gently, massaging the last few drops out before I let go and flatten my hands on the wall behind me.

It takes all my energy to push myself upright. I wince and turn away from the stream to let my semi fade away while I finish a cursory shower.

I'm still woozy with happiness by the time I make it out to the bedroom. I grin slowly and sit on the edge of the bed, closing my eyes. Holy hell, the things I want to do to this man blow me away.

Then I pick up the phone and see Caleb's answer.

Can't wait.

I laugh softly to myself and finally force myself to get dressed again, this time in something decent I can wear for the date this evening.

Yeah, me neither.

CALEB

It doesn't bother me that Tag goes quiet in the middle of my lunch break. I have a sneaking suspicion I know what's keeping his hands full, and it makes me shiver with delight.

I love knowing that he wants me. I might even be brave enough to experiment some more tonight. But I'm not brave enough to lock myself in the office bathroom while I explore those thoughts, so I have to push them away for now.

It'll be worth the wait later.

I'm spending my lunch hour at my desk instead of going to a coffee shop with my coworkers. It's not an accident, either—I packed a sandwich and a flask of coffee this morning.

Today, I have something to keep me busy.

I might not be able to quit my job and live as a traveling poet right now, and maybe people are just being polite and pretending to like my poems, but that doesn't mean I should give up on writing new material. I can keep trying to do better.

This morning, when the alarm stirred me from a delightful dream about Tag, I decided that I'm going to work hard at this. Once a week, I'll stay here and write poems instead of spending an hour nodding and making sympathetic noises while coworkers talk about their kids.

It's a quiet little office, with just ten of us working here. My corner of the office is tucked by the window that faces the street. I've covered the windowsill with plant pots, and the cubicle walls in photos from the Black Claw trails and parks further afield in Vermont.

When work gets stressful, I can look up at a little piece of nature and let the other part of my brain out to play for a moment. Sometimes I'll even stare at the stark beauty of nature instead of the computer screen while my fingers move on autopilot through spreadsheet fields.

That's where most of my poetry comes from: imagining myself there and yearning for something I can't quite touch from what feels like as far away as possible.

It's not a *bad* place to work. It's just... a cubicle, and there aren't a lot of good poems to write about cubicles. Trust me, I've tried.

Hunched over the page as I scribble words and cross them out, I lose track of everything around me. I've already set a timer for ten minutes to one o'clock so I can get ready for my coworkers to return.

There are no great works of art coming out of my brain yet, but it's been a while since I really sat down and focused on writing poems instead of writing only when inspiration strikes.

I rest my chin on my fist and stare into space at my cubicle wall as I try to keep my attention. I'm trying to write a poem about the tasting room, but everything just comes out sounding like a real estate description.

I want to capture the essence of last night: delicate flavors bursting on my tongue as we explored each other, both before we started kissing and after. Maybe what I'm really trying to write is about that kiss.

Oh, man. What a kiss.

I've kissed guys, usually while drunk at the bar on New Year's Eve. It's never been like this. This time, I didn't find myself wondering what's so attractive about lips smushing together.

I was too busy losing myself in worlds I didn't even know existed within my head, enjoying the flames bursting to life within my chest and the desire that welled up.

Fire? Fire and alcohol? And wooden barrels? There's got to be some image there I can work with.

But it's so hard to form words when all I want to do is write volumes about Tag's eyes and the way his eyes crinkle a little at the edges when he smiles, and how surprisingly soft his beard is.

God, everything going on in my head is amazing. I want the whole world to know how incredible Tag is and what he does to me.

"Did you forget this?"

I nearly leap out of my skin. My boss is standing behind me, holding a printed page.

Shit. I started this lunch break by typing poetry before deciding that I'll do better handwriting it. I must have hit print and forgotten about it in my eagerness to let the ideas flow.

My cheeks flush. "I don't habitually print personal material on the office network," I promise him solemnly.

Gary is a good guy and he's usually pretty laidback. I don't think he cares, but I still feel like I've been caught texting in class.

He laughs. "I waste more paper every time the damn thing jams. Don't worry about it, kid." Then he leans past me to set the page on my desk and claps my shoulder.

Oh, God. He read it, didn't he? I fix a smile on my face and pray that he goes away, right now. Maybe vanishing into the floor? That would work.

But he doesn't. In the kindest voice possible, Gary says, "Don't quit your day job yet, though, huh? We need you here."

"Uh huh," I mumble.

But instead of deflating totally, I just remember last night—the depth of passion in Tag's eyes as he listened to me read my work. *He* believes in me. What Gary just saw was my warmup exercises, not my finished work. Embarrassing, but not representative of my skill.

"I wasn't planning to," I promise him. "But I don't want to end up like a kid who skateboards on the same leg all the time. You know, all numbers, no creativity."

Gary looks surprised for a moment as he leans on the cubicle and bites into an apple. "Not a bad analogy," he admits when he swallows. "But I used to be an artist, you know?"

"You?" Then I turn crimson with embarrassment. I didn't mean to sound so disbelieving, but Gary is the kind of guy who wears the same three colors of button-down shirts all the time. He never struck me as an artist. "Sorry."

He's not offended. He just chuckles and throws the apple core in the trash, dusting his hands off. "Yep. You've got some talent, don't get me wrong," he nods at my warmup exercises again. "But nobody told me until I got into a mountain of debt from an art degree that I couldn't paint for shit."

I don't want to laugh, but his grin invites me to laugh with him, so I do. "Oh, no."

"Yeah. I hate it. I liked screwing around drawing cartoons, and I thought a fine arts degree was my ticket to a syndicated comic strip." Gary rolls his eyes. "Luckily, accounting saved me, and now I'm here."

I wait, wondering if he's still drawing those cartoons, but he doesn't offer up any more information. There's not even an inspirational tale about doing what you love on the side.

He just smiles expectantly at me, so I smile back at him. "Yeah. Good thing I love numbers."

Gary chuckles. "Sure is. Anyway, I'll send you the new client's file after lunch, huh? Enjoy the rest of your lunch."

"Thanks," I mumble, rolling backward to watching him head back to his office and close the door. Then I let out a sigh and scoot back to my desk before pressing my forehead against my notebook.

I'm tired of people trying to save me from mistakes *they* got to make. And that answers my other pressing question: whether I should answer my brothers' group chat texts about how last night went.

I texted them good morning, so they know I'm alive. And it's normal for us to go a few days without talking to each other. They can deal with their curiosity for a little while.

I just want to give this a fair shot with Tag before I start reporting back to other people. I don't want them analyzing our relationship, like what we have can be entered into a spreadsheet.

Maybe it's a mistake, but it's about time I followed my heart. Whether I'm falling in love or falling over my own ass remains to be seen, but I don't think that's the point.

Romance isn't about the destination. I've been focused on that for too long. It's about the journey, and for the first time in my life I'm just relaxing and letting things unfold without second-guessing myself.

Nobody is going to get in the way—not yet. There's too much sweetness to enjoy first.

TAG

Considering how long I've been living here, I don't get out much. This is my first time actually eating in the Maple Factory, even though it's right next door to Vino and Veritas on Church Street. Usually I dash in, grab a maple donut, and run.

Anyone I want to meet for business, I bring my wares to their bar or restaurant. And I don't have a lot of friends locally, mostly hiking buddies I just meet on the trails.

Truth be told, I've spent a lot of time avoiding being in public, too. Years of dodging paparazzi and trying to get groceries without being interviewed can take their toll.

Now that I'm meeting Caleb here, I feel strangely like I'm connected to the town at last, and nobody is pointing or staring. I'm nice and anonymous, but people still smile at me on the way in and hold the door.

"Thanks," I say and hurry through, looking around. Caleb isn't here—phew. No keeping him waiting this time.

It's a cute little bakery and café, and exactly the kind of place to make my stomach growl as soon as I walk through the door. It might surprise people to find out that I don't have that much of a sweet tooth, considering what I do. Just as well, or more honey would wind up in me than in the mead.

But a maple cruller from this bakery? Oh, I can make an exception for them.

As I hear the door opening behind me, the hair on the back of my neck tickles just right. I know who's here before I even see him. I'm already grinning as I turn around.

"Well, look who showed up."

Caleb gasps and pretends to look for the watch he's not wearing. "You beat me!"

"I've been waiting hours, you know," I tell him, keeping a perfectly straight face. "My feet are falling off."

People nearby hide their smiles in the way you do when you see a couple on a date, and that makes me even happier. I have to agree: we're obviously cute together.

"You're lying," Caleb accuses me.

And for a moment, the gulf in my chest opens once more. My heart races as I swallow down my panic. He doesn't know. He can't know. He can't out me in public!

Caleb jabs me in the chest with his finger as he playfully scowls. "I saw you park your truck."

See? My worries come to a screeching halt, and I swallow down my second thoughts once again. I laugh, hoping it's not as shaky as it feels. "Damn. Busted."

Before he can notice anything amiss, I turn away to lead us to a table. "Over here?" I choose one next to the window and pull back a chair for him.

I love how flustered he looks when I spoil him, so it only makes me want to do it more. Sure enough, Caleb shyly folds his hands in his lap as he sits down. "Thank you."

"You're quite welcome," I murmur, leaning down a little as I push his chair in. My breath ghosts over his skin, and I can't miss the goosebumps that pop up in response, or the eager hitch to his breathing.

"Now, what can I get you?"

His eyes shine up at me. "A maple cruller, please and thank you."

"And to drink? Coffee?"

Caleb stares at me. "Oh, no. I like sleeping. Green tea, please."

I chuckle. "Green tea it is," I agree, keeping my thoughts on the beverage to myself. Then I head up to the counter, glad that there isn't a line. We've come at the quietest time, it seems. There's only one other table with a young couple talking intensely.

Once I've ordered the crullers and two cups of green tea—despite my misgivings, I'm prepared to give it a chance on Caleb's word—I return to the table and settle down across from him. "Here we go."

"Thanks."

The war in my head isn't getting any easier. If I tell Caleb, I'm risking him outing me to the whole town. It would shatter my peaceful little life here.

But maybe I don't have to give him the whole speech now. I could just tell him I used to be in a band or something. No need to tell him *which* band.

I don't know him well yet, but I think I know him enough. If I ask him to keep a secret, I trust him to do it.

But before I can say a word, Caleb stares at me like a deer caught in headlights. "Um… oh, God. Sorry."

"For wh—"

A big hand lands on my shoulder. "Hey!" The voice is friendly enough, but not one I know. I turn and look up at the guy standing next to us.

No question about it, this is one of Caleb's brothers. They have an eerily similar smile, but of the two of them, Caleb won the hotness lottery. This guy is dressed in a suit and tie and shiny shoes in a town where not many people just go around dressed like that.

Caleb said one of his brothers was a lawyer, didn't he? I think I'm about to meet him.

"You must be Tag." The guy sticks out a hand to shake. "Elijah. Or just Eli."

"Hi." I take his hand and shake it, then try to stand up, but he waves off the formality.

"Oh, don't let me bother you two." Contrary to his words, Eli seems determined to bother us, because he grabs a chair from the next table and turns it backward, plopping down to grin at us both. "I just wanted to introduce myself since I was passing by."

This guy has a big personality, the kind that fills a room. If his brothers are anything like him, I suddenly understand why Caleb is so quick to turn into a wallflower.

"That's nice of you," I agree with a placid smile. I risk a glance at Caleb, who looks like he wants to disappear into a hole. "It's good to meet his family."

Truth be told, I'm flying blind here, but I really want Caleb to like me and he does seem to value his family's opinions. And it *is* a little weird for his big brother to suddenly show up for an inter-rogation.

Poor guy. It's starting to make sense now why he feels like he can't strike out on his own.

Caleb peeks up at me. "You don't mind?" he asks with a mouthful of cruller.

I really don't. It surprises even me. But nobody can choose their family, and it could be a lot worse. Like, Eli could be an actual ax murderer in the woods.

"Nah," I assure him.

Eli tilts his head as he looks at me. "You look familiar. We haven't met, have we? Normally I remember faces," he adds, apologetically. "Tag, is it?"

"No, no. Don't worry. I don't think we have," I assure him, smiling as I try to keep the panic inside. "Just Tag." I'm sure as hell not telling him my full name. The last thing I need is for Eli to turn out to be a Jet Slack fan.

"Phew. I never forget a client. I don't want to break my record." Still, he eyes me like he's trying to see my jawline underneath my beard. Which is exactly why I let it grow out—so that I'm a lot harder to spot.

It still happens sometimes, especially in big cities. But here in Burlington, I've been hoping that after years out of the spotlight, people will just assume I'm part of the background scenery.

To derail that conversation before it can go entirely the wrong way, I smile. "Caleb's told me lots about his family. It sounds like you all get along pretty well."

"Yeah," Eli says and grins. "We've heard about you too. But I think our Caleb was planning to hide you until the wedding."

I laugh gamely, but Caleb turns scarlet and mutters, "*Eli.*"

Eli raises his hands and gets up. "Okay, I'll leave you two love-birds to it so I don't scar him for life."

"Too late. About twenty-odd years too late."

"True. And I've got all the embarrassing stories to prove it," Eli tells Caleb and reaches out as if to ruffle his hair. Caleb dodges, so he chuckles and waves to me, then says, "See you, kid."

"*Bye,*" Caleb says pointedly. Once the door closes, he drops his forehead into his hand and rests his elbow on the table. "I'm really sorry. I told them not to do that."

I just chuckle and reach over the table, offering him my palm. "I know what brothers are like. They'll keep teasing as long as you're shy about it. But you've got nothing to hide. How about we give them something to *really* gossip about?"

Caleb's eyes widen as he looks up at me. Then he smiles slowly and shifts so he can rest his palm in mine instead. "Thanks," he whispers.

I wink. "Just gaze into my eyes like we're..." I twirl my fingers through the air, miming a fork. "Sharing a bowl of spaghetti."

Caleb's lips twitch like crazy. I can tell how hard it is to hold in the giggles. "Please don't mime spaghetti."

Oh, God. Now I want to crack up, imagining us sucking up thin air and mirroring each other's movements. I bite my tongue hard.

Neither of us look around, but out of my peripheral vision, I can see him stumble to a halt on the other side of the window.

"Slurp," Caleb whispers.

Oh, no. I can't hold it inside anymore. My shoulders start to shake as Eli hurries past us. Just in time, because I crack into loud laughter.

"*Caleb*," I manage once I catch my breath. "Man, don't do that. I think I broke a rib."

Caleb snorts with laughter, which only sends us both into another fit of laughter.

"Oh my God, the group chat will be *wild*." Caleb grins at me when we finally calm down. "Thank you. They're all worried that…" he trails off, hesitant.

"That what?"

He turns a funny shade of pink and raises his green tea to his mouth. From behind the cup, he mumbles, "You want to get into my pants."

I raise an eyebrow. That explains the protectiveness. "I do. But that's not all I want from you."

"I know," Caleb murmurs. Then he smiles shyly and reaches for my hand again, laying his palm lightly on mine.

It makes my heart go all kinds of funny, and I find myself stunned into silence, gazing at him. He doesn't look away. And this time, we're not just teasing.

I swallow hard, my pulse racing. His green hues have caught my attention and pinned it down. I just want to scoop him up in my protective embrace and give him the confidence to stand up to everyone.

He's beautiful. All he needs is to be himself.

"It's nice that they care about me getting hurt, but it's getting a little ridiculous." Caleb shakes his head ruefully. "I just want a fairytale romance without everyone breathing down our necks."

"Yeah," I whisper, and I finally squash down the guilt. "I know what you mean."

Thank God I didn't tell him, then. He's going to think that I want some guy to be in the spotlight with me. And maybe I used to want that. Truth is, these days I just want a guy who drags me into the corner of the party and steals my heart.

So far he's doing a pretty damn good job of that.

After meeting Eli, I'm pretty sure he could wrangle the details out of Caleb and then my identity will be all over town. Better to keep both of us safe from everyone else's expectations for a little while longer.

"Just the two of us," I promise aloud in a murmur.

Caleb smiles and scratches my palm gently with his fingernails. Oh, God, the sharp sensation sends my brain screeching to a halt, a line of fire shooting directly down my spine into my dick.

Not so sure about sitting next to the window now. But Caleb obliviously keeps tracing circles over my palm, and it feels so good in deep parts of my brain that I don't want him to stop.

I sip my green tea and then make a face. Yeah, I'm not a convert. I think it must be a healthy person thing. I'm healthy, but not so healthy I want to sacrifice my taste buds.

Now that the cup is cool enough, I drain it fast to get it over with.

I try my hardest to keep my reaction inside, but Caleb laughs at the face I make. "That's a no to green tea, then. I won't judge you too harshly."

"Strictly coffee for me."

"Even this close to bedtime?"

I'm torn between two answers—the nice, polite one, and the one I *really* want to give. But after a moment, I realize that Caleb's giving me a sly little grin. Waiting to see if I take the opportunity.

I could tell him that coffee doesn't really keep me awake—but I can't tell him that years of sleeping when and where I could on the road seemed to do that to me. So instead, I choose option B.

"Bedtime isn't *that* close," I murmur. "I'm sure they're closing up soon here. Do you wanna… head somewhere else?"

"How about my place? It's just a few blocks away."

Yes! I was hoping he'd offer. I'm endlessly curious about Caleb, and there's no better way to get to know someone than to see where they live. "Awesome," I agree. "No nosy dogs to interrupt us."

Caleb giggles. "Perfect," he agrees and drains his cup of green tea. Then he eats the last few bites of his cruller and licks his fingers clean.

Very thoroughly and slowly.

Okay, I'm only a weak mortal. Try as I might, I can't stop myself staring at Caleb, memorizing the sight of his pink tongue running around his digits.

Suddenly my shower fantasies are back, and they're a hundred times more intense playing out in front of my very eyes.

My cheeks go hot, and my ears are buzzing until I almost can't hear his next words.

"Ready? I'm all done now. Let's go."

"Yup," I manage, shifting in my chair to zip up my jacket *before* I stand up. Luckily it goes down to mid-thigh—and I wore dark trousers today.

"If you don't mind a little walk," Caleb adds, his eyes sparkling like he knows exactly what trouble I'm having. When I cast a little look his way, I notice that he's wearing a baggy sweater that goes to mid-thigh. Fashionable but also practical, I now see.

"I don't mind," I tell him and lace my fingers with his, stepping out into the cold.

The breeze is actually a relief, and though it makes me shiver in discomfort, it helps me get a little bit of self-control again. As eager as I am to jump into bed with Caleb, I'm curious about the shift.

Yesterday he was all about romance, but now he's hinting at other desires, too. Did a few kisses change his mind about waiting until he gets to know me better?

I really want to know what's going on in Caleb's head. Before I jump his bones, we have to talk.

Better now than never.

CALEB

"I'm not gonna lie," Tag tells me frankly as we wander down Church Street hand-in-hand. "You're sending me a lot of signals right now, and… I wanna make sure we're on the same page."

For once, he looks nervous. His grip on my hand is tight and a little bit damp.

"Oh?" I lick my lips, squeezing his hand. "About what we want?"

"Yeah." Tag's voice is just a little bit hoarse, and I suddenly realize how much of an effect I've been having on him.

Holy crap. Behind all those muscles is a whole shitload of pent-up desire, and I think I'm going to pop with how much I want to unleash it.

"I want…" I swing our hands as I try to figure out what to say. "I want us to be comfortable with each other."

"Mmhmm." His brows draw together as his gaze flickers away across the street.

"I want to know that you aren't just gonna use me and forget my number next week."

Tag catches his breath and gives me a look of concern.

"It's not—that hasn't happened to me before. No traumatic

Grindr stories here." I blush and clear my throat. "But I guess… I'm struggling to figure out what *you* want."

"What I want? Or what I want from you specifically?" Tag asks, his gaze perceptive.

My mouth goes dry. "Both, I guess? Like, what is it about me that you want, if it isn't just sex." Before he can answer, I quickly raise my other hand. "Honestly, I'm not looking for compliments."

Tag nods slowly, his brows pulling together. "You seem like you're confident in who you are sometimes. But other times, not so much. I haven't figured it out yet."

Really? It's simple, in my mind. "I am who I am," I tell him frankly. "I'm a giant nerd. A little bit flamboyant, and not ashamed of it. I'm not trying to tone myself down for other people's sake. I'm not going to pretend to be someone I'm not just so that you'll like me. I'm only ever going to be… me."

Something flickers through Tag's eyes. Silence falls for a few long seconds as he catches his breath, like he wants to say something. Then he bites his lip as he squeezes my hand. Whatever it was, the moment passes and he just smiles. "I admire that."

"Thank you." Then I grin sheepishly. "Although I have considered it, because I'm really into you."

He laughs softly. "I'm glad you didn't. I'm into you because of who you are."

Oh, God. I want that to feel amazing, but we're bumping up against that wall once again. "Which is…?"

"Talented, sweet, smart, funny…" Tag trails off, shrugging. "I know you don't want compliments, but it's the truth."

My mouth dries up. "Who I am and what I do are like, different things." I can tell I'm getting close to the truth, because there's a strange lightness in my chest. Like the burden eases when I speak it aloud. "I know who I am. I just don't… believe that person could be destined for greatness. Does that make sense?"

A breath rushes out of Tag's lungs, fog rising through the air. "Dude. You really don't see it?"

I blink at him. "See what?"

He comes to a halt and takes my other hand as we stand under a streetlamp, and I feel for a moment like we're in the big moment where he confesses his love for me.

Too soon, I scold myself.

But Tag startles me. "I think you have talent. You should do more with it. Don't stop at one open mic. Submit your poetry different places, do more live readings. Let yourself grow."

Okay, in its own way, those three little words are even better than the ones I was picturing. "You really… believe in me that much?" My head is spinning again, and we haven't touched a drop of booze.

"Of course," Tag murmurs, tilting his head as he gazes down at me. "Don't you?"

I don't know how to answer that. I gaze at him for a good minute as I try to sort through the tangle of emotions in my chest.

I'm grateful for his faith in me, even if I'm kind of puzzled. All he's seen is me stumble my way through a reading—largely thanks to his help—and then a one-on-one reading when we were both too drunk to care how good my words were.

"I'd like to," I finally whisper.

Then we turn and keep walking. The silence between us is comfortable, like Tag is just giving me space to think about every-thing. Which is a good thing, because boy, do I have a lot on my mind now.

"And for the record," I finally say once we're on the landing of my apartment, at the top of a narrow staircase. I fumble for my keys, blushing as I slide them into the lock. Then I look at him. "I want you. I just don't know what's supposed to come next."

Tag smiles, brushes his fingers along my cheek, and rests his hand gently on the back of my neck. "Screw what's *supposed* to happen. Whatever you want, that's what we'll do."

I swallow hard, push open the door, and turn around so my back is pressed against it. Then I reach for his hip and pull him against me, and his weight presses against me.

"I want you."

13

CALEB

I'm going to die of happiness.

Heat floods me from head to toe, and my head spins as Tag's hard body presses me up against the door. The air in my puffy jacket slowly deflates under the pressure of his body, making me giggle.

He grins at me in that confident way—maybe a little cocky, but in the fucking hot way and not the irritating way. Then he grabs both of my hands, dragging them over my head as he laces our fingers together.

Pinned here by him, my knees melt. If not for his body anchoring me where I am, I'd start sliding down the door.

"Hello," Tag whispers, his breath a hot maple gust across my cheek. Then he kisses me and I forget my own name. His lips are a hard, hot crush. I just want to yield and let him sweep me off my feet.

"Nnf!" I finally squeak when he pulls away and lets me catch my breath. My lungs don't seem to work, and my cheeks are burning.

Tag's breath is warm on my kiss-swollen lips. His eyes are gorgeous pools that I could just lose myself in.

"Now, shall we lower your heating bill?"

I blush furiously. "By getting under the covers?"

Tag's lips twitch into a mischievous smile. "I was thinking of closing your front door." He lets go of my hands, and they slide down until they rest on the top of my head.

"Oh." I snort sheepishly as Tag winks at me. "Yeah. That's not a bad idea."

It takes a moment to peel myself off the door and step inside after him. The door swings closed on its own, which is good because I can't quite remember what I'm supposed to be doing.

Tag stops me from fumbling with my jacket and pockets by stepping closer. He gently pulls the zipper down, sliding the coat from my arms. Then he turns to look for somewhere to put it.

"That's the closet," I point to it. "Allegedly. I've never been there."

Tag tips his head back and laughs, and I grin at the bare, smooth curve of his throat. God, every little thing about him is beautiful.

As he hangs up my jacket and his own, I twist my hands together, trying to get a grip. "I should offer you a drink or some-thing. But I really just want to make out right now. I'm a terrible host."

Tag closes the closet door and turns to lean against the hallway wall. "Then I'm a terrible guest, because I agree." He slides his hand along my shoulder and down to my hand, pulling me close.

I try to dig in my heels, but he's too strong. I stumble into his chest with a laugh, and he wraps his arms around my waist. "Gotcha."

"Yeah, you do," I mumble into his chest, pressing my forehead against his shoulder.

"Hmm?"

"Nothing." I clear my throat as I find my balance. He's doing that thing where he gazes at me from a few inches away, his eyes flickering across my face and landing on my lips like he's plan-ning what to do to me. "I might just turn into jelly if you kiss me like that again," I warn.

"Can't have you fainting on me."

In one swift move, Tag flips us around and I hit the wall with a gasp. Then he leans in, capturing my lips in another fierce kiss that makes heat burst in my cheeks. He slides his teeth along my lower lip as sparks flash through my veins, and then the tip of his tongue seeks mine, firm and insistent.

He explores my mouth recklessly. There's no gentleness and precision—only the uncontrollable passion swelling between us.

"Yes," I gasp when he lets me catch my breath, his eyes dragging up and down my body. Then he pushes his knee between mine to hold me in place. One hand glides over my curls, scrunching them as he cups the back of my head. The other glides over my chest.

My heart thunders at the dull touch of his fingertips and the pressure of the heel of his hand. I need more already.

"Good?" Tag purrs, that confident little smile on his lips again. He leans in, nipping my earlobe, which makes me cry out and quiver. The sting shouldn't feel so good, yet it shoots straight to my core as all my muscles go taut.

"Mmmph," I moan. "Please…" I don't know what I'm begging for, but my body sure does.

Tag's hand slides down my chest toward my stomach, and the most ferocious need thunders through my brain, drowning out all thoughts.

Now, I beg him silently, arching away from the wall and grinding against him.

The hard line of my cock is trapped between my hip and his thigh, and the heat through my jeans is a whole new kind of friction. It's a dizzying high I never knew about until this moment.

I need more, now.

My pants are suddenly so tight. My cock is trapped inside, straining against them, twitching and aching like crazy. My head is spinning with the full force of years of fantasies suddenly playing out in real life.

Another man is about to touch me for the first time in my life, and I want it *now*. I've craved this forever, and my body approves of the risk my heart has finally taken.

I playfully tip my head back to brush the tips of our noses together. "Like what you feel?" I murmur.

"*Love* it," Tag corrects me, his voice a sensual growl. He presses a string of tiny, teasing kisses against my lips, pulling back every time I try to deepen it.

Oh, fuck. I couldn't be happier that he's in charge. This is a hundred times better than I'd hoped for.

The heel of Tag's palm presses against my waistband. My shirt has risen, and his fingertips rest on my bare belly. I giggle and squirm, but he just presses firmly and grins.

The tentative, nervous excitement floods my body with a hot, tight energy. We're tumbling forward, pushing toward an edge I've never experienced, but I'm ready to take the plunge.

There's no second-guessing it. It's happening.

"Can I?"

"*Duh.*" I flush with pleasure. I'm glad he's asking. It's sweet and caring of him, and it makes me feel like I'm in safe hands. It's also a way of teasing me, and it's working.

"Hmm. Not sure I heard you." Tag grins, sweeping his hand up over my belly.

I grunt. "Nnnnnh-no," I mumble, pouting up at him. "Please." Sure, it feels incredible to feel the heat of his palm against my bare skin. But it's impossible to ignore throbbing heat trembling through my shaft. It's going to hurt soon if he doesn't do something.

"Yeah? We can take it slowly if you want." His fingertips find my nipple, and just one flick across the sensitive nub makes me cry out as my knees buckle. I desperately loop my arms around his shoulders and press close to him.

It takes me a minute to catch my breath. "B-Better not," I gasp. "Or I'll really embarrass myself and jizz in my pants."

Tag relents and glides his palm down again, and all of a sudden the pressure of his palm cups the line of my hard cock.

"Well, that wasn't hard to find." He pinches the shaft between his thumb and fingers, tracing the outline in my trousers.

"Fuck," I grunt, my eyes squeezing shut. I'm already wet at the tip, leaking precum in my excitement. The dull pressure isn't enough. I need these layers of clothing off.

That means moving somewhere it's easier to get undressed. "Couch?" I gasp, pushing forward into his hand. I force my eyes open, licking my lips as I shiver in pleasure.

It's hard to think about anything that isn't crazily grinding against his palm. Suddenly, the idea of dry-humping is really fucking appealing. Anything to keep my body in contact with his.

Tag winks. "Right here was fine with me, but if you want to be classy… you'll smarten me up."

He gently steps back, taking hold of my hips.

"Wh-What—" I stutter, adrenaline leaping into my throat. He's walking me backward all of a sudden. I try to turn to see over my shoulder, but he won't let me. He leans in to catch my lips, giving me a playful little kiss with every step.

"Fuck," I gasp and give in at last, letting go of my worries and letting him steer me.

It's worked so far, hasn't it?

"Wait," I gasp when the familiar surroundings of my living room come into the periphery of my vision. "The coffee table."

"No problem." Tag scoops me up in his arms like I weigh nothing, and then tosses me onto the couch.

I hit the soft surface and bounce, laughing in mock-outrage. "Like a sack of potatoes!"

"No," Tag growls and swings his knee over me, straddling me sideways on the couch. "Of sugar."

"I don't know if I'm all that sweet." I try to play it cool, but Tag's hands are roaming up my shirt, and every drag of his skin on mine makes me gasp.

"Let's find out."

I groan my agreement and grab the front of his shirt, fumbling with the buttons as he does exactly the same with me. Our wrists clash against each other's as we playfully fight to be the first to undress each other.

"There," Tag growls when he reaches the last button just before I do. His shirt hanging open above me, I can better admire his body.

"So fucking hot," I gasp. My bare palms touch his chest, and it's just as firm and hot as it looks. I run my hands down his chest and belly until I hook my thumbs into his belt loops. "Kiss me."

He fulfills my request instantly, shifting his weight forward and crushing me with his weight so that his lips can touch mine. I gasp in delight, quivering as the line of his hard shaft meets mine. Every shift of our bodies makes us grind together.

Holy fuck, it feels incredible. I wasn't kidding about not lasting long. This is entirely different from me and my hand—or, for a treat, me and a pillow. No, this is a thousand times more sensation, even with all our clothes in the way.

"Nnngh," I grunt when he bites my lower lip and plucks at it. I try the same move on him, and I'm rewarded with a delicious, deep groan.

My hands can't stop wandering, exploring the heat of his chest. My fingertips against his nipples make him shudder against me, thrusting his hips to grind our arousals together.

When Tag pulls away from my lips, he nips my jaw, licking his way over to my earlobe. I don't expect the degree of pleasure that strikes when he reaches it and wraps his lips around it, flickering his tongue rapidly across it.

"Fuck!" I arch clean off the couch, my thighs shaking as I struggle to breathe. Somehow, a line of hot fire seems to shoot straight down to my dick, and I can imagine the tip of his tongue on me...

"Touch me," I gasp. "*Please.*"

I don't have long, and I can't wait anymore.

"Yes, boss," Tag murmurs playfully. He kisses the side of my neck and then my collarbones. Everywhere his lips touch flares to life, sending more pulsating bursts of heat through my body.

Especially through my cock, painfully hard and tight.

One of his hands fumbles with my trousers, unfastening and unzipping. Then he slides his fingers through the opening at the front of my briefs, and his fingertips make contact with the over-sensitive skin.

A senseless cry leaves my lips. My feet press against the couch as I push myself against him. "Fuckfuckfuck…"

Tag pushes all the layers of clothing down so that my cock can stand straight between us, and at the same moment, his lips close around my nipple.

I can't even manage words anymore. I cry out hoarsely, scrabbling at his shoulders as heat pumps through my body. The wet heat of his lips and tongue drag around the little nubs of my nipples, back and forth between them.

His big, firm fingers wrap around my cock, and my breath comes in little panting cries. I try to thrust into the tight circle of his fingers, but he's doing all the work for me. His hand twists around my shaft, dragging and gathering all the sparks until they pool there, then pulling back up to the tip.

Every stroke of his hand drags me closer to the edge, and I'm already fighting to hold on. I gasp his name—or something close to it—as my nails dig into his back.

The grunt of pleasure he gives makes me grin and do it again, deliberately scratching from his shoulder blades down to the small of his back. That's all I can manage, though. Even words are still off the table.

My whole body is too tight and hot. The blackness is sweeping closer like never before, and all I can do is choke out a whimper of warning.

Then I'm lost.

I throw my head back and buck against Tag's hard body as he pulls me apart at the seams and wrings out every drop of ecstasy from my depths. My balls draw tight and then heat floods through my shaft and the rest of me, right to the fingers and toes. My mess splatters between us with every stroke of his hand.

As I go soft, he lets go of me and steadies himself on my hip.

Then I realize his other arm is moving, and I gasp and wrench my eyes open. He's kneeling over me and stroking himself, the pink head of his shaft appearing from his tight fist with every pump of his hand.

"Holy fuck," I groan. I'm spellbound, watching him pleasure himself. His face is flushed pink, his eyes glassy and lips parted.

"F-Fuck… Caleb…!" Tag gasps and clutches at my hip. I slide my fingers into his instead, letting him crush them in his grip.

"Come for me," I whisper, licking my lips. I'm fixated on the sight. I've never seen anything this hot in my life. "Show me everything, Tag."

His cry rings from the walls as he throws his head back and bares his throat, his hips stuttering into his hand all of a sudden. Then time itself seems to freeze for just a moment, his hand wrapped around the base of his thick shaft.

And he spills his load. It's not just *spilling,* either. The first squirt shoots through the air, and I gasp and instinctively blink. His thick, white mess falls short of my face, but it coats my chest and belly.

I grin with delight, squeezing his fingers. "Yes," I whisper. "Oh, you're beautiful."

Tag sways where he is, helplessly thrusting into his hand as he wrings himself dry. "I… I can't believe it," he grunts. "How hot you are."

My toes curl as I beam up at him. "Speak for yourself. Jesus. Wow. If this is taking it slow, we can pump the gas now."

He laughs hoarsely and collapses on top of me, and I nestle into the weight of his body crushing me into the couch.

Then he kisses me, finally soft and tender again, and I close my eyes to bask in the moment.

This was everything I've ever hoped for and then some. It was incredible, letting down my walls and placing my trust in Tag. And wow, did he ever spoil me. My heart is about ready to burst with joy.

"Well, that's modern art if I've ever seen it. Got a cloth?"

I burst out laughing and point him to the bathroom, but secretly, looking down at myself is so hot that I kind of want a round two already.

Turns out a filthy, delicious, delightful part of me loves being marked—or claimed, possessed… whatever you want to call it. Or maybe it's just because I know it's all Tag's and mine.

Whatever. I love it.

Good things come to those who wait.

14

TAG

If there were a prize for biggest smile, Caleb would win it. He's grinning at me just like Queenie. It makes me laugh, but I can't stop stroking his shoulder and playing with his curls.

We're dressed again, and we're on the couch. He's lying down with his head in my lap, looking up at me like he can anchor me here if he tries.

Which he is. I'm determined to stick around for a while, cuddle him and talk. Just to make sure that Caleb knows I'm not about to forget his number now that I got off.

Getting a glimpse in Caleb's head isn't easy, but I think I'm starting to figure him out. He's confident in who he is, but not confident that anyone else wants that.

It makes my heart ache. Who *wouldn't* want someone like him, honestly?

But he's also been overprotected for his whole life. I don't think he's learned to trust his intuition—about what he wants or about what other people want.

But I know exactly what I want—I want to date this guy. So I'm going to make myself clear and make sure there can't be any misunderstandings.

Caleb closes his eyes and hums as my fingertips run in gentle circles around his scalp. "Have you dated a lot of people before?"

Apparently I'm not the only one thinking along these lines.

"Slept with, sure," I tell him and chuckle. "Dating? Real relationships? No, not really. I traveled a lot, which lends itself to hookups. I didn't want roots anywhere before I moved here. I wanted to chase the quick thrill."

Caleb cracks his eyes, watching me thoughtfully. For a moment, I'm expecting him to ask and I'm bracing myself to explain it all.

I should tell him. I really should. If this relationship is going somewhere, it's not going to stay in the past forever.

But I don't want him to think of me differently. I just want what we've got to continue. It's not the right time yet—but I'm not going to lie, either.

"Do you regret it?" Caleb asks, and I stifle my sigh of relief.

"No. I learned a lot about myself and the world."

"Like what?"

I let my fingertips wander from Caleb's hair down the side of his neck, and then idly scratch his chest. "Like… the value of having something solid and steady to ground you in all of life's ups and downs. Working hard but relaxing hard, too. Being present, however much it hurts."

"Mmm." Caleb rests his hand on top of mine, tracing my knuckles. "I've often wondered if I made a mistake, staying a virgin for this long." He says the word with a little wince, like he's expecting me to comically overreact.

It wasn't like I hadn't guessed. So I just smile at him. "Mm?" I encourage him to go on.

Caleb lets out a tiny, relieved-sounding sigh and closes his eyes. "Everyone makes it out to be a big deal, especially when you're in your twenties. Like it's this big rite of passage and you should be past it by now."

I shrug. "Sex is just sex. God knows I love it," I grin. "But it just tells me you had other priorities."

Caleb nods, the back of his head sliding on my thighs. "Exactly. My priorities were my family and career. I always thought my relationship history shouldn't be that interesting—it's the present that matters. The past is boring."

I shouldn't take it as permission... but I do.

"Yeah, exactly. I want you to know me for who I am *now*," I murmur, sliding my fingers into the spaces between his. I don't have to tell him everything yet. I'm just testing the waters. "You get to experience all the things I've learned from sleeping around. I get to experience all the things you've learned from not wasting your time on assholes. Men, right?"

Caleb bursts out laughing. "That's a good way to look at it." He gazes up at me again, then nuzzles his cheek gently against the back of my hand, and I think I might die of how cute he is.

"Yeah. And neither of us have had serious relationships before," I point out. "We're both flying blind. And I don't want to rush this. But I do want to keep... walking along a path that might lead that way."

Caleb snorts with laughter. "Yeah. Let's keep hiking. It's a deal."

Good. We're on the same page. I really like this guy, but before I can call myself his boyfriend, I think we need to spend more than three glorious days getting to know each other.

At least one more day, right?

"And I'll keep going slow," I promise. "If sex isn't important to you, we can work with that. I like sex a lot, but relationships are about figuring out what the other person needs."

Caleb makes a strangled little noise. "Whoa. Just for the record, I'm very, very interested in getting laid."

He startles me yet again into a laugh. I love that he says what he means and takes me by surprise.

"But if you're seeing to my needs, you could make me a sandwich," Caleb giggles, playfully reaching up to poke me.

"Okay." I grin down at him and ease my thighs out from

under his head, pulling myself to my feet. "Let's see what's in the fridge." I stride over there and pull it open.

Finally, Caleb murmurs, "Tag? I didn't expect you to."

"I know," I say with a smile. He's still lying there, staring at me with his brow furrowed like he's solving a puzzle. "That's why I'm doing it."

"Oh." Caleb pushes himself to sit upright slowly, a hand rising to the back of his head, absently pushing his hair around. His eyes are shining now, a smile playing around his lips as he watches me.

The fridge is exactly as neatly organized as I'd expect. There's a shelf that seems to be devoted entirely to sandwich ingredients, so I pull everything out and start opening cupboards to find plates.

"Above the toaster."

"Thanks," I tell Caleb. "Any preferences?"

"Lots of butter, a little mayo."

"Got it." It makes me happy to do this little thing for him. Anything I can do to show him that he deserves to be spoiled and looked after.

As I make two sandwiches, I notice that Caleb isn't saying much. I wonder what's going on in his head. But that's all right—maybe he just needs a minute to get used to the idea of someone spoiling him.

I sit next to him, passing over one plate. "Here you are."

"Thank you," Caleb murmurs softly. The way he gazes at me makes me blush, and then he leans in and presses his lips against my shoulder. "This feels… good."

"Good," I tell him. My chest glows with pleasure at hearing it. It's so special to me that Caleb trusts me with his body and home, and his first times. "Tell me if it ever doesn't, and I'll do the same. I think that's all we need to do, right?"

"Mmhmm." Caleb grins. "God. I don't regret the past, but all of a sudden, I feel like I've got years to catch up on. Is that weird?" He rests a hand on my arm, his eyes barely leaving mine.

I hunch awkwardly over the plate, afraid of dripping mayo

onto his couch. "Nnh-nnh," I mumble around a bite of sandwich. Once I've swallowed, I shake my head. "Does it feel like we've known each other for years?"

"Yeah. Yeah, exactly." Caleb still isn't eating his sandwich. His fingers wander gently up my arm. "Thank you. For… being so open."

That hits my belly so hard that I can't breathe for a moment. *Should I?*

No, my brain tells me in almost the same moment. How would I even begin that conversation? *So, hey, baby… speaking of being open, I've got my own Wikipedia page?*

Those big eyes make me want to move the world just to rescue him, but I think the only threat right now… is me. Or rather, the person I used to be.

I envy Caleb a little bit, and admire the hell out of him. He's always been true to who he is.

But I'm different. If he knew that I sold my soul, and wrote and sang a bunch of stuff I don't believe in… I don't think he'd respect me. And that would kill me.

He has to get to know who I really am first.

"Eat your sandwich," I tell him. "Before I get distracted yet again."

"Do I distract you a lot?" Caleb picks up his sandwich as he grins at me.

"Constantly. I've lost so much sleep over you already."

Caleb laughs. "So there's something that *does* keep you up."

I smile and look down at my plate, swallowing my next bite of sandwich despite my suddenly tight throat.

Oh, he has no idea.

CALEB

I've been dreading this moment for hours. It feels like we could stay up all night talking—and I want to. But at last, I can't keep Tag distracted forever.

He slips his phone out of his pocket and glances at his screen. My heart sinks as he sighs. "I guess I should go feed the mead."

That wasn't the excuse I expected. I just stare blankly at him for a moment as my brows pinch together. "Like, bring it a sacrificial offering of ravioli?"

Tag laughs so hard he starts coughing. I grin and wait patiently for my explanation, patting his back. "No," he finally manages. "The yeast in my new batch. I feed it nutrients to keep it fermenting."

"Which means…" I narrow my eyes. "More alcohol?"

He pauses like he wants to explain more, but then gives in and laughs. "Yes, more alcohol."

"Well, I thought you were just escaping spending the night with me," I tease him. I hope he can't hear the nerves in my voice. "But I guess that's an acceptable excuse."

Tag pauses and tilts his head as he runs his thumb around my knee. "I guess I am," he admits finally. "I wasn't sure if that would be too much too soon for you."

It feels like nothing could ever be too much or too soon with Tag. But I can't say that without sounding desperate.

"Nah," I say carefully. "I'd like it. Though... I do have to get up for work."

Tag shrugs. It's hard to read his face—like he's keeping it studiously blank. "No problem. I could drive you back here early. Or you could show up in yesterday's clothes and be the talk of the office for the rest of the week."

Oh my God, is he actually agreeing to this? "I'm not dragging you out of bed too early?"

"I was gonna drop off another case at V&V anyway. It's really fine, Caleb. I can survive one early morning." He winks. "For a good cause."

But under his cool exterior, I'm starting to catch glimpses of excitement. He wants this—he's just trying not to pressure me.

Aww. How sweet. Meanwhile I'd climb him like a kitten rides a Christmas tree to the fuckin' ground.

I catch my breath and rest my hand gently on top of his, flattening it against my knee. As I watch him, it feels like the world just shifts a little bit.

My heart and head agree on where we're going.

"So? May I expect the pleasure of your company?" Tag teases me, sandwiching my hand between his.

I giggle and slap my other hand on top. "Sure. Let's do it. As long as I get a taste of *something* to reward me for going out into the cold night."

He grins and stands up. "You didn't specify a taste of what. But I certainly wouldn't take advantage of that."

I pretend to gasp, but a little thrill races through me. *I want to suck dick for the first time.* "You'd better not take advantage of me. That would be simply terrible," I flirt for my life, resting my hand against my forehead.

Tag grins knowingly, takes my hand, and pulls me to my feet. "Deal. A taste of mead in the moonlight."

I have to bite my tongue to stop myself from squeaking as the romantic in me melts into a happy puddle.

When I can breathe again without embarrassing myself, I practically sprint for the door. "Let's go."

It turns out that feeding mead isn't very exciting. I'm more interested in looking around at the steel and plastic kegs all over the place. The concrete floor and plain walls couldn't be more different from the tasting room, and it feels like a behind-the-scenes sneak peek.

As Tag connects pumps to the huge steel tank, I wander over to the windows at one end of the meadery and admire the view—inside and out.

It's interesting to see him in his element, trudging around the place in old rubber boots. I noticed he offered me the newish-looking ones. Apparently sometimes disasters happen, and he didn't want me ruining my shoes.

Intriguing, but I'm glad no disasters have unfolded. Today has been perfect and I don't want it to go wrong now.

When I turn my back on Tag and look through the long window at the end of the building, the view is almost as entrancing. A beam of moonlight from the crisp, dark sky illuminates a small lake in the rolling field.

"That's all my land, up to the trees," Tag says from close to my ear, startling me. I'm tired, and the beautiful view totally distracted me for a moment.

He smiles, puts an arm around my shoulder, and reaches in front of me. In his palm, he's carrying two tiny tumblers, hardly bigger than shot glasses.

I carefully accept one and he shifts the other into his fingertips, raising it to his nose.

I copy him, and then do my best to muffle my cough a

moment later as the alcohol fumes rush into my lungs. It's a lot stronger than the ones I tasted before.

"Easy does it," Tag coaches me with a chuckle. "Just a little sniff. Hmm. That's what he said?"

I choke with amusement and elbow him, but he looks remorseless while I splutter my way to breathing again. "Okay, Mr. Fancypants." This time, I inhale just a little bit with my lips open.

I'm greeted by a whole meadow of sweet floral scents, which is weird when we're staring out at the dry, brown grass of late autumn. If the sky weren't so clear, it's cold enough to snow, and the moon is steadily rising across the distant pines.

I tip the glass back and sip, moaning with delight. There's none of the heat I was expecting. This is a fruity, floral, sweet drink, kind of like I was expecting when I first thought of mead.

And it's really nice, like a glimpse at a hot summer's day despite the cold winter moon illuminating the landscape.

I shiver and burrow into Tag's arm, and he frowns with concern and rubs my shoulder. "Warm? Need another layer?"

"I caught a chill coming in from the truck." I give him an over-dramatic sigh. "Better get some fire into my veins."

"Mmhmm. A nightcap straight from the tank. That is *also* not a euphemism."

This time I'm ready for his innuendo, and I can contain my snort. "Tell me about this, then."

"Just a simple show mead. Honey, water, and yeast—that's all."

I glance down at the glass in my hand. "Really?" It tastes like he's added all kinds of summer flowers and fruits.

"That's the honey. My girls work hard," Tag says with a distinct note of pride in his voice that makes me smile. "I've hand-trained them to go for the best-tasting stuff."

I eye him, and by the twitch in his lips, I know I've caught him in another lie. "Stop pulling my leg."

"Oh, is that your leg?" He bumps our hips together. "That wasn't what I was aiming for."

I laugh and shake my head. "So dirty a man. So clean a mead. How'd that happen?"

"Magic," he shrugs. Then he smiles and tips his head back, slowly sipping, and I copy him.

We both stay quiet as we finish our glasses. The moment feels special, gazing out over the lake. There's a stone bench out there. If it weren't so freaking cold, I'd suggest sitting there to look at the stars.

But we can stay warm and see them from right here. I can even forget the quiet gurgle of the pump running in the background.

"This *is* magical," I finally murmur, handing him back my empty glass when he holds out a palm. "I can see why you love doing this."

The corners of his eyes crinkle with pleasure. "Yeah. It's a dream come true."

I smile and turn to watch him as he lets go of me, heading back over to put the glasses in the industrial sink in the corner and turn off the pump.

"Let's go to bed before it turns back into a pumpkin," he suggests, rejoining me.

My brow crinkles as I put a hand on his arm. "That's not how the story goes."

"It's our story," Tag says, so softly I almost miss it. Then he flicks the lights out and leads us outside.

I swallow hard, my heart thumping against my ribcage. It takes my breath away to think that he's right. That we get to write our own story. At last, I've found everything I've been waiting for.

I'm too tired to look around at his house very much. It's close to eleven o'clock now, maybe even midnight. We just head straight up the stairs. At the top, the staircase opens up into a spacious master bedroom stretching across the whole floor.

The blinds are open, and Tag moves to close them, but I shake my head. "It's pretty," I murmur. I like watching the moonlight shine through the window. "Nobody can see in, right?"

"We're all alone here," Tag promises. He flicks the lights off, and then I hear him undressing.

I sit on the edge of the bed to do the same, any nervousness gone. I forgot to bring pajamas, but I think Tag will happily keep me warm tonight.

My eyes adjust after a minute to the shape of him moving toward me in the darkness, carefully joining me on the other side of the bed.

When my clothes are neatly folded on the bedside table, I pull back the warm comforter and crawl underneath, snuggling up close.

This first moment of being pressed up to him, naked from head to toe, isn't awkward at all. Not after having shared so much intimacy earlier.

It's the most natural thing in the world, turning so my back's to him and he can wrap himself around me. His warm, fuzzy arm slides over my side, and his hand gently rests on my chest as I put a hand on top of his.

My back is pressed against his chest, and every breath he takes gently whispers across my skin.

It's all so very new to me, yet within minutes it feels as comfortable as anything.

Fairytales do come true.

● 16

TAG

When I wake up, I'm smiling before I even know why.

Then I open my eyes to the sight of Caleb's curls, his body still tucked against mine after the whole night together. My dick has something to say about that.

But then I shift and frown. His leg can't be over mine, not at this angle.

Then the lump on my legs moves, and I sigh and peek over the edge of the comforter.

Big brown eyes look back at me. Queenie tilts her head and grins at me, her tail softly thumping on the comforter. There's no door in this house that can keep her out.

Now that she knows I'm awake, I have about sixty seconds to get out of bed or the chaos will start.

"Quiet," I whisper, my voice hoarse. I clear my throat and scoot away from Caleb while Queenie stands up. Luckily, I manage to extricate myself without waking him, and then the race begins.

Will I get dressed before the Lab starts barking?

Underwear, jeans, T-shirt, socks—warn Queenie to stay quiet again as she jumps to the floor…

Yes! I made it.

She leads the way downstairs, and I take a moment to look behind me once more. I wish I could have slept in, just to draw out these precious moments a little longer.

But at least I can make him breakfast in bed before work.

Caleb looks angelic, asleep in the rumpled sheets with his curls all over the place. The pink rays of dawn's light stream in through the room, lighting it up in that beautiful early winter way.

Queenie makes a quiet chuffing sound that I know means she's about to start barking, so I hastily shut the bedroom door and walk downstairs as calmly as I can.

Despite my best efforts, when I get to the bottom of the stairs, it's all over. She can't stop her excited barks before I manage to get the front door open. The harsh sound echoes off the walls and all through the old farmhouse.

No way is Caleb still asleep now.

"Thanks, girl," I say with a sigh, but her excitement about a new morning is always infectious. I can't stay mad at her. When she comes in again, I fill up her bowl with kibble and set to work on our breakfast.

It doesn't take long for my smile to return. I hurry to grab things from my pantry: a loaf of organic bread from the little place on Church Street, and a carton of eggs from the farm down the road.

Breakfast might be simple and quick, but at least he'll know that I'm trying. I'll save the pancakes and hash browns and sausages for a weekend.

Maybe, if I'm very lucky, this weekend?

I *am* lucky already.

I can't believe how life works. I just happened to drop off that case of mead at the right time. Instead of keeping my head down and fleeing for my cold truck and warm home, I was ready to look around—and Caleb caught my eye.

And it's not all luck on my side. He got up so much courage to perform for the very first time that night.

I just wish it had gone better. Well, *I* think it went great, but he's clearly embarrassed.

If only he had another chance...

Wait. Why doesn't he?

Telling Caleb that I have faith in him makes him bolder. I can do even better, though. I can talk to Tanner and organize a little event to spotlight Caleb. I'd coach him through it, or share the stage—whatever he needs to feel comfortable.

I know he can do it. He's captivating, and his work is beautiful. It deserves a bigger audience than just me and Queenie.

I've been standing here with the fridge open, my hand on the butter, for way too long. I distractedly pluck the foil-wrapped block from the fridge and nudge it closed with my toe.

My mind is racing. I've been thinking about ways to get more locals aware of the Silver Crown brand name. If sponsoring an event boosts mead sales at the bar, Tanner wins too.

I know how to hustle for gigs. It wasn't all slick radio hits and acting the part of the obnoxious rock star. If I show him what I learned from that part of my life, he might not judge me so much for... well, for selling out.

I can help keep Caleb from selling out or giving up. I'll be the wind beneath his wings. Maybe he'll end up performing or publishing a book of his poems. Who knows?

He needs someone in his life who believes in him unconditionally. I want to be that man.

There's literally no downside.

Queenie barks as Caleb's footsteps on the stairs warn us of his approach. "Good morning," he greets a moment later, smiling as he crouches by Queenie for a cuddle.

"Oh, I see how it is," I laugh, but I'm not offended.

"I'm saying hello to the mistress of the house first."

"And then her loyal and obedient servant," I point at myself with a grin.

"Bingo." He winks and straightens up, slipping around the breakfast bar to stretch onto tiptoe and kiss me good morning.

"Mm, good morning," I whisper against his lips and kiss him back. Then I remember I started heating the stove for the eggs. "Oops. How do you want your eggs?"

"Over easy?"

"Done," I salute him with a spatula.

Caleb sits down at the breakfast bar, blushing adorably. "Breakfast? You're spoiling me."

"It was going to be in bed, but Queenie had a lot of loud thoughts."

Caleb grins and looks around my house. "It's gorgeous here."

"Thank you." My chest swells with pride at the admiration in his glance, but I'm impatiently waiting for my chance to bring up my idea. "So, I have an idea…"

Caleb raises his brows, so I draw a breath and launch into it. "Would you consider trying another event if I were there alongside you the whole time? Coaching you, helping you practice, whatever it takes."

Caleb's eyes go wide, but not with fear or annoyance. He actually looks touched. "You'd do that for me?"

"Duh," I tease and wink before grabbing plates. "I'd be really happy to organize that. I can talk to Tanner and set something up."

Caleb draws a breath and lets it out. He bites his lip. "Only if you're there with me again."

"Of course," I promise, meeting his gaze as I switch off the heat to the stove. "Every step of the way."

He smiles so much that dimples appear in his cheeks. "I'd love that, then. I think I can be brave again if you're there."

"Yes!" I nearly drop the toast in my excitement, but recover it just in time and flip it onto the plate as he giggles. "Awesome. I'll set it up today."

"How come you're so good at public speaking? Can you really help me get better?"

The toast is getting buttered pretty hastily. I want to distract him before we go down this road. "I promise it gets easier. Every business owner starts out nervous. When you've pitched a room of potential clients..."

"Oh," Caleb laughs softly, accepting my explanation with such ease that I almost feel a little guilty.

I'm not lying, exactly. Omitting the full story, definitely. But I don't want to live in the shadow of my Google results and tabloid photos and the whole damn life I left behind.

Ironic, really, that Caleb thinks I'm the brave one. If only I could have been the real me all along, I never would have gotten into that mess. But then I wouldn't have run away here and met him...

Meant to be? I sure hope so.

"Here you go," I say, a little too loudly. I slide the plates across the breakfast bar with a flourish, then sidestep around it to join him on the other stool.

Breakfast doesn't take long, unfortunately. These last few, precious minutes fly by in what feels like seconds.

Then I grab a case of mead and hop in the truck with Caleb to drive him back home. This time, I leave Queenie at home because I'll have to track down Tanner.

But first, I have to say goodbye to Caleb for another long day or more. My spirits sag as I pull up outside his apartment and apply the parking brake. "Here we go. Your carriage has arrived, sir."

Caleb smiles and unbuckles, sliding across the seat toward me. "Thank you for an amazing night."

"No, thank you." I smile and cup his cheek affectionately, my heart twinging. I don't want to let him go.

For God's sake, it's not like we're saying goodbye at the airport. But all my heart knows is that we're parting. And now we've had a taste of what it could be like... it's going to be hard to spend a night alone.

"I'll see you soon," Caleb promises, like he knows what I'm thinking. Then he kisses me once, pressing his lips against mine. "And I'll text you even sooner."

I grin. "I'll hold you to that," I murmur, my fingertips slipping free from his hand as he slides out of the truck and waves. I raise my hand for a wave and watch him go into his apartment.

Now it's time for the plan.

When he's gone, I get out and lock up the truck, then hoist the case of mead into my arms.

Tanner lives above the bar, so he might be around—he doesn't seem to sleep. I don't think it matters whether I talk to him at seven in the morning or at night, he'll still reply in as few syllables as humanly possible.

If Tanner isn't awake yet, I'll drop off the case with one of the guys at the bookstore… and then text Tanner to make sure none of the bottles take a hike. I know those bookish types.

But when I knock on the back entrance, I'm happy to find Tanner himself pushing open the door. He grunts, tips up his chin, and reaches for the case in my arms.

"Hey, uh, can I ask you something?"

He shrugs. "I'm here."

I bite back a smile. He's not that grumpy, really, he just doesn't say much. And I can respect that. "Can I run a little event?" I ask. "I was thinking Silver Crown could sponsor Caleb for a little poetry event… call it, I dunno, Bees and Beats?"

The name is terrible, but Tanner only raises a brow for a moment. "Knock yourself out. How's Monday?"

"Perfect." That's probably their slow night, so we can bring in a little extra business and everyone wins. I grin and just manage to stop myself from shaking hands since he's still holding the case. "Awesome. Thanks. I'll print out some posters and drop them off."

He grunts again and nods, and then I turn to head back to my truck, whistling under my breath.

Everyone wins. How perfect is that?

It feels like I'm going back to my roots, when we first formed. Way back before success bred its own problems, I was always the guy hustling for gigs. I was the youngest by a few years, and some bars insisted on drawing Sharpie Xs over both my hands if I played there after nine o'clock or something dumb.

God, that feels like a different lifetime now. Long enough ago that it's a fond, pretty funny memory instead of a sharp pang making a home in my gut.

I keep whistling all the way back home, where I greet Queenie and wash up the breakfast dishes, before I realize what tune is playing in my mind.

It's another old Jet Slack song I haven't even thought about in years.

I dry my hands off, and before I can think twice about it, I head down to the cellar. There's a few boxes I've never unpacked, and I know exactly which one I'm looking for.

I blow the dust off the lid, then ease it off the white carton. I pull out a few handwritten pages, hardly able to breathe at how familiar it all seems.

Holy crap. I can't believe I kept this stuff. I ditched nearly everything—or let them auction it as part of what I call the divorce agreement. At least some fans got mementoes, and I got the money to come out here and start my new life.

Pretty much all I kept was this box. It's all the rejected lyrics.

I remember the arguments like they were yesterday. I wanted to take Jet Slack a different direction, stop doing the same thing over and over. Start being *real* again, like we were before we lost our way.

But I guess I was the one who'd lost my way. I was the odd one out.

Not even as the gay one. They were fine with that. But they were happy to live that life, smashing up hotel rooms and getting the hottest girls in the club.

I played along, sometimes. I didn't like when they blew our money on losing our hotel deposits, but when they went looking for hot girls, I found hot guys. I kept up in the clubs, shot for shot, bottle for bottle.

I was young, stupid, and I deserve every word in my Wikipedia "Personal life" section. But... I can't keep pretending I *wasn't* that guy, either.

Maybe I can dust off that part of my life and put it to work now that there's a good reason. If Caleb's brave enough to show himself to the world every day, I can spend one evening revisiting my own past.

It's time to see what I left behind.

CALEB

Tag knows how to tease a guy.

He texted on my lunch break to tell me that he's got a surprise, but he won't show me until I'm home from work. Part of me thinks it's an excuse to get on the phone with me, but I'm totally willing to play along.

I thought a day apart from Tag would feel a year long, but daydreams keep me captivated and the time flies by in a haze of reports.

I can't stop wondering what kind of surprise he means. The sexy kind? I really hope it's the sexy kind. Like candy underwear, or a well-composed dick pic to save in my Hidden photo album.

I've got a one-track mind today.

I'm glad for the desk and my tightest underwear hiding the shape of my thoughts. It's technically ten minutes to quitting time. Gary doesn't seem to mind that everyone else plays fast and loose with our working hours, so my coworkers just left.

I just have one more sheet of numbers to transcribe, which should take up the next ten minutes. And then I'll be free, too.

But ten minutes feels like a lifetime. Every time I glance at the clock, the minute hand hasn't moved. And when I double-check my spreadsheet, I spot a few sloppy mistakes.

For once, my brain has checked out early. It's too fixated on the memory of last night.

I can't shake the visual, clear as day: Tag kneeling over me, one his strong hand curled around his cock as he grips my curls in his other fist. Okay, maybe I'm embellishing the memory, but I love him playing with my hair.

My fingers tap on my number pad automatically as I glance around casually, like anyone's here to see. I slide the other hand onto my lap, my palm resting on the bulge of my shaft.

My cock jumps under the touch, and little sparks shoot straight to my toes. I press harder, dragging the heel of my hand slowly over my erection.

Jesus, I'm so hard it hurts. So close to the edge already. It wouldn't take long…

I sprawl a little bit in the chair so it looks casual, my gaze flickering to the window.

Someone would have to look inside at just the right angle to realize. Even then, they wouldn't see anything…

No, my common sense kicks in at last, and I bite back a whimper as I look at that page. But there's no way in hell I can do this while I'm so distracted.

You know what? Fuck it. It's time to let myself play by other people's rules. I'm always here ten minutes early. I'll just do this in the morning.

"Caleb?"

I gasp and throw my hands in the air like I've been caught stealing. Not that I've ever tried, of course. Too much of a goody two-shoes.

Oh my God, I'm a nerd. I hastily run my hands through my hair and try to breathe. "Yeah?" I lean around the edge of the cubicle, ready to roll toward my desk again in a hurry.

Gary stops on the other side of the office, car keys in hand. "Everyone else is gone. You nearly finished?" he calls out.

"Yeah. I'll lock up in a minute," I promise automatically.

He smiles and gives me a thumbs-up. "Don't stay too long."

Gary's the good kind of boss who doesn't let us do unpaid overtime.

"I'm going right now." As soon as I can walk home without poking an eye out. Maybe I should have said "coming in a minute."

"Right on. Catch you tomorrow."

I hold my breath, waiting for the office door to rattle, swing closed, and rattle again with the sound of Gary locking it.

Then I reach out for the blinds, twisting them closed. My heart thuds in my ribcage.

Heat pulsates through my cock as I roll back toward my desk again. I can barely breathe as I shut down my computer.

As the screen goes black, I draw a breath.

Just do it.

Before I can second-guess myself, I plunge my hand into my pants and underwear, cupping my aching cock. Pleasure washes through me, the oversensitive nerve endings finally satisfied—but not for long.

"Fuck," I hiss, every sense on high alert. I know for a fact there's nobody left here, but still...

This is beyond daring for me. This is the boldest thing I've done in my entire life, and there's no stopping it now.

My thighs quiver as I hurriedly unzip my pants and thread my erection through the fly. I gently cup my balls with my fingers, freeing them too.

The very tip of my cock just brushes the underside of my desk, which is cool and firm.

Oh, God, I'm turned on.

I can't help staring down the length of my body. My shaft is illuminated by the harsh overhead light over my shoulder, standing out in the dark under the desk.

Oh, the things I want Tag to do to me.

I brace my feet on the floor as I curl my fingers around my shaft, tugging from base to tip. It's awkward, making sure I don't smack my wrist on the edge of the desk.

But holy fuck, am I turned on already. My body is tight, every muscle screaming for more *right now*.

So I indulge, rolling backward with a quiet gasp as I set into a hard, fast rhythm. I don't leave myself a single moment to fantasize and draw it out.

This is sheer need flooding my body. I'm jerking off like I want it all to be over in seconds. No time for shame or second thoughts. Only for indulgence in the fantasy playing out in my mind.

Tag, bracing himself over me, one hand in my curls, the other around his huge, straight, veined cock...

Guiding it between my lips. I choke as the head of his cock slides all the way over my tongue to the back of my throat, whimpering in delight. I can just about hear Tag grunt with ecstasy as I desperately suck my cheeks around him.

Every time he thrusts his hips, fucking my mouth, wet and frantic noises of pleasure escape from my throat and vibrate through his stiff cock.

The chair squeaks under me as I stop trying to muffle the harshness of my breathing. I pant for breath, spreading my slick precum over my shaft.

My muscles are so taut that I feel like my whole body might snap.

"Fuck," I gasp, my back arching and head rolling against the backrest of my chair. "Fuck, fuck..."

It's coming, and there's no stopping it. I quickly sweep my arm over my desk, pushing away keyboard and papers alike. Then I stare down at myself, my lips parting as my whole body seizes and my balls draw tight...

Heat floods through my shaft and slams into my body. The strength of my voiceless cry makes me bare my teeth as breath rushes from my lungs.

My whole body contracts in such hard pulses that my feet leave the floor and my knees hit the desk for a second. There's no containing the mess. The sprays of hot, thick passion land on the desk and my shirt and pants.

I crush myself into my chair, squirming with the force of the tidal wave washing through me. My chair slowly pivots toward the window, but I hardly notice.

If anything, I can picture Tag waiting for me after work on the other side of that window.

And it's *amazing*.

"Fuck," I whimper at last as my body starts to go limp, my feet touching the floor as I melt into my chair. I'm hot and sweaty and strangely… mellow.

Then my brain starts to clear, and I giggle softly at the situation.

When I'm tucked back in my pants, I take a good minute for cleanup, dabbing my shirt and pants clean. Good thing my jacket will hide those spots until I'm home.

My cheeks flush, and I walk with an extra little strut as I finally leave the office and lock up for the quick walk home. I can't stop smiling with my own little secret.

Oh, Tag. What the hell are you doing to me?

I'm glad I cleared the pipes before calling Tag. I might still be a little giggly, but at least I'm not initiating phone sex.

Yet.

"So here's the surprise. I've asked Tanner, and he approved an event next Monday. A little poetry reading. I'll feature you on the poster: local poet Caleb… what's your last name?"

"Holt. Yours?" I ask, laughing softly.

He hesitates for a moment and then snorts. "Nothing fancy. Campbell."

"Cool," I murmur distractedly. Is Caleb Campbell too weird?

"Local poet Caleb Holt," Tag continues, unaware of the fairytale endings dancing around my brain. "Sponsored by Silver Crown. Everyone wins."

At last, my brain catches up. "Wait, did you say Monday?"

"Yeah. I thought the longer you wait, the harder it'll be. You only build it up as this mountain in your head."

Okay, he's right there. After weeks of planning, I only grew more terrified of open mic night. Maybe if I do it as soon as possible, I'll remember what he taught me about staying calm and reading to one person.

"How do you like the plan?"

"I love it." That much is honest, surprising even me.

"Thank God," Tag groans. "I was worried you'd hate it. Or me. Maybe both."

"Never," I promise, my hand rising to my chest. I'm lying on my back on the couch with the phone to my ear like a lovesick teenager. "As long as you don't leave me alone up there."

"No way. I can stay up there with you. Or even read out some of my own writing. Only if you want."

I gasp. "Yes! You write, too?" He kept that quiet, all right.

"Used to," Tag says with another self-deprecating snort. "That's the real surprise, right? Who didn't have an angsty soulful phase? Don't worry. I've been rated solidly mediocre. The warmup act is there to get people excited for the pros."

I giggle breathlessly. "Thank you," I murmur sincerely. I love that he's willing to stick his neck out and look like an idiot to make me feel less alone. And I'm helping Tag spread the word about his business.

"We're in it together. Deal?" Tag asks.

"Hmm," I hum playfully. "One condition."

"Name it."

"Dinner with my family before you make me famous. Sunday?"

I can actually hear Tag gulp, which makes me grin. "Are you sure?" he murmurs.

Oh, crap. Is this too soon? Maybe he wants to take his time to decide whether I'm boyfriend material, without the pressure of my family.

"Very. Unless you don't want—"

"No, Caleb. It's not that I don't like you," Tag cuts me off firmly, and I smile with relief, dragging my hand down my face as the stress vanishes. "It's just that your family all seem… scary accomplished."

"I know," I groan. I'm glad I'm not the only one who feels inferior in comparison. "But they're nice, don't worry. They just want to protect me."

Tag hums and I cringe, hoping I didn't just scare him off. But before I can walk back my suggestion, he seems to make up his mind. "All right. Any price to pay for another date with you."

I grin to myself. "We don't have to wait until Sunday for that."

"Well…" Tag chuckles. "Saturday is supposed to be the first real snow of the year. A couple of inches. I was thinking we could spend the day together?"

A whole day with him in a romantic winter wonderland? I'm in heaven. So many times, I've imagined walking hand-in-hand along the snowy streets with a gorgeous guy of my dreams.

Now it could actually come true.

"Yeah," I whisper and roll onto my front, pulling the phone away and squishing my face into the pillow to muffle my excited squeaking noise.

Tag's talking about ideas, his voice sounding hollow from the speaker. "—sledding if it snows enough, or walking around town. Or we could stick to my land. There's lots of snow there—"

I finally manage to contain myself and clear my throat, pulling the phone back to my face. "Your place," I decide. "And you can pick me up that morning as soon as the roads are clear."

Tag laughs. "Aye aye," he teases. "You're in charge."

"I am. But so are you," I murmur.

"Yeah," Tag murmurs. Then a series of sounds in the background make me raise my brows. "Shit," he mutters. "I need to look at that pump. Text you later?"

"No problem," I say, trying to sound casual as I squirm around the couch with happiness. By the time he texts, I'll probably still be lying here staring into space and planning our kids' names.

After our goodbyes, I press the phone against my lips like I'm kissing him good night, my cheeks heating up.

I might be a lovesick fool, but it's intoxicating and heady and… strangely empowering. Knowing that Tag wants me is like the ultimate elixir. And boy, oh boy, do I want him.

Saturday can't come soon enough.

18

TAG

The phrase "snow angel" was invented for Caleb.

I may be hopelessly infatuated with him, but I'm pretty sure that anyone with more objectivity would stop and stare, too.

He's dressed up in his puffy blue jacket and big furry black boots. He refused to wear a hat when I offered him one, so his golden curls are gathering snowflakes.

And I can't stop myself thinking romantic shit like, *He's the ice prince of my heart.* I'm not giggling, but he is—a lot—and it makes me grin until my face hurts.

God, I'm screwed.

"There," Caleb pants and turns his head left and right, trying to work out how to get out of the snow angel.

I grin and skirt around him to his feet, trying not to mess up the pristine snow he threw himself into. I can probably reach over and grab his hands to help...

The loud bark doesn't give either of us enough warning.

"Queenie, no!" I shout, but I'm too late. She's already launched herself through the snow at Caleb, hitting his stomach with a solid thump as she wriggles all over the place, no doubt thrilled that he's down here on her level.

"Help!" Caleb laughs, trying to cover his face while she licks him like crazy, rolling onto her back and flailing through the snow. "Argh! My ears! Not the ears!"

I'd help, but I can't breathe. Not because the air is too cold, either. I'm just doubled over laughing, my hands braced on my thighs. The more I laugh, the more excited Queenie gets, and the more she mauls Caleb.

Finally, Queenie peels herself away from Caleb and lunges at me, barking at my knees before she goes tearing away through the snow toward the lake.

"Don't—" I trail off and throw my hands in the air. There's no stopping her now.

She hits the water with a splash while Caleb just stares up at me, damp and mussed up and perfectly adorable. "What just happened?"

"Chaos. The living embodiment of chaos, that's what."

I crouch by Caleb's side and grab his wrist as he clutches my shoulder. Together, we manage to pry him out of the snow angel. It's pretty messy and surrounded by paw prints now, but in my eyes, that just makes it all the sweeter.

Once he's on his feet, he staggers into me and wraps his arm around my waist as I brush his curls out of his face again and try to dust the snow off them. Snow is already melting down the back of his neck, making him flinch and giggle.

I'm so freaking happy when he's around. I've barely thought about work at all. It's like rediscovering a version of me that I thought was long gone—all playful and relaxed.

Caleb rubs his hands together briskly and blows on them, but they're still so pink that I wince.

"Give me your hands," I tell him, turning my palm up. When he rests his ice-cold fingers in my hand, I cup my other hand on top and rub vigorously.

A strange series of noises draws Caleb's attention, and he twists to look over his shoulder. "Is Queenie all right?"

"Yeah. She's probably harassing the ducks. Keeps trying to make friends with them."

Caleb laughs and looks back at me. "She's running back to us with the world's biggest log."

Sure enough, when I look behind Caleb, I snort. I don't know where she found a branch that size from, but it's dragging through the snow as she trips over it.

"You need a full-time dog sitter," I tell Queenie, but as usual she's proud of the chaos. She drops the branch proudly at my feet and sits, grinning and wagging her tail furiously. It swishes through the snow like she's making a snow angel of her own. Snow dog-butt.

She looks at the stick and then me. "I'm not throwing it for you. I haven't actually trained as a caber tosser."

Caleb, who's taking a photo of his snow angel, giggles and snorts.

Queenie barks and runs between us, then shakes herself off. This time I join in the cry of dismay as ice-cold water droplets fly everywhere.

I groan and bend over to drag the branch over to the firewood pile. When I turn around, something makes impact with my chest.

My jaw drops at the splatter of snow on my chest and the mischievous grin on Caleb's face. He crouches in the snow, already scooping up another handful.

"This is not the Ides of March, and I did *not* warm your hands so you can stab me in the back!"

"The chest, technically," Caleb retorts, hauling his arm back with another snowball.

I only just duck in time for it to soar overhead, smacking into the side of the lean-to where I store the firewood.

Adrenaline rushes through my body as I drop to a crouch and run my palms through the burning cold layer of snow at my feet. "Oh, it's *on!*"

Caleb might be cute and all, but I'm not letting him nail me in the face. *Not this way, anyway.*

"Get back here, you…!" I exclaim as Caleb scurries for cover behind the garage. I'm hot on his heels, flinging my hastily-crafted snowball. It falls apart, and I curse.

"Amateur mistake. You obviously didn't study the art of snowballs," Caleb pants as he shapes another ball in his frozen little hands.

"And you did?" I finish mine first and fling it at his shoulder, but he flinches backward and it smacks directly into his chest, snow spraying up under his chin.

Caleb squeals and falls backward as guilt floods me. I haven't hurt him, have I? I should have been more careful. "Oh my God, are you all right?"

"That's really fucking cold!" Caleb exclaims, but I only realize it's a trap too late. All of a sudden he brings his arm up and retaliates with a snowball of his own that bursts against my shoulder.

"Wounded!" I exclaim and clutch my shoulder, staggering backward. "By trickery!"

Caleb's giggling like crazy, hopping to his feet. He looks around, but there's no chance to get away. Not the speed I launch myself toward him.

As gently as humanly possible, my hand cupping the back of his head, I bodyslam him against the garage. "Enough," I growl.

"*Yes*," Caleb moans and rolls his head back against the wall. I can't feel the warmth of his body against me with this many layers of clothes, but he's firm and eager against me.

Heat flushes me, my heart suddenly thumping with delight. I intended it to be playful, but Caleb didn't even bat a lash. He pushed it into a realm I didn't intend, and now I can't shake the arousal that's flooding my veins. Doesn't help that he's grinding against my thigh, a faint smile on his lips like he knows just what he's doing.

"Mmmph." I bite back a groan of frustration. I want him so much that I can't make the right words come out.

No need for words. Caleb tilts his head back and parts his lips in an invitation. I roughly card my fingers through his curls, brushing the snow off. Then I pull him in for a kiss, devouring his mouth.

Queenie gallops closer, barking sharply. Then she butts the back of my leg with her snout.

As air rushes back to my lungs and my brain switches on again, a tiny giggle slips from Caleb. "I'm okay," he promises her. "This is our idea of fun."

Damn it. Queenie's wide, adoring eyes are definitely puncturing the mood—but that might be a good thing.

"Whew," I pant against Caleb's mouth and gently let go of his hair, touching his cheek instead. "Let's go warm up."

"Let's," Caleb purrs.

I can't tell why he's mischievously smiling, and my eyes narrow suspiciously. A moment later, I have my answer. The twin icy blocks of his hands are on the back of my neck.

He wriggles loose from my grip and trots for the house with a big grin that diffuses any trace of annoyance I might have felt.

I want to let him get away with everything. All of it. More than I even know how to guess at right now. I've found paradise, and it wasn't just this place or this life.

Paradise is Caleb's smile.

19

CALEB

The crackling log fire in Tag's stove is music to my wet, freezing cold ears. We pull off our wet outer layers, and though I'm tempted to keep going, I match Tag and stop after the socks come off. For now.

"Not that I'm commenting on the oral hygiene of your dog, but I'm going to wash my face," I inform Tag. "Where's the downstairs bathroom?" I only know the top floor of the house.

When he's done laughing, he points me to it and I excuse myself for a quick splash of warm water and hand soap. I've never been so thoroughly mauled in my life. But despite Queenie's exuberance, I love being around the man and his dog.

It feels like I fit just right into their life—as they do into mine. It's *fun*. I feel light and relaxed and happy. And despite the chill in my bones, my heart is full to bursting at the prospect of cuddling up on the couch by a log fire on a snowy winter's day.

"Hot chocolate?" Tag greets me when I emerge. He's got mugs and a milk carton on the counter.

"Ooooh, you *are* spoiling me. Yes, please."

"Find yourself a seat, but I recommend against the armchair. Prepare to be invaded."

"Like, in the butt?" I grin, looking over my shoulder as I pad across the hardwood floor to the lounge.

Tag drops the spoon on the ground, then curses and bends to scoop it up. His cheeks are red when he straightens up again and grunts at me. "You know what I meant."

"I hope I do." I bite my lip hard to keep myself from laughing, but I take his advice and steer away from the armchair. Instead, I settle on the couch in front of the fire.

I expect a damp Queenie to join me, but to my relief she's looking perfectly innocent in her fluffy dog bed next to the fireplace. She's napping and drying off from her adventures.

"Good girl," I murmur and earn a sleepy tail thump. She cracks her eyes, probably checking if there are treats with those words. When she sees there aren't, she goes back to sleep.

A sleek knitted blanket is folded on the back of the couch, so I pull it down to wrap half around my shoulders, leaving the other half for when Tag joins me.

It's a beautiful house, and the living room is no exception. Tag isn't the stereotypical bachelor with bare light bulbs and a couple of mismatched throw pillows. No, he's taken his time to make this place feel like home.

The floor is hardwood, and the coffee table is a light wood with curved legs that matches the dining room furniture on the other side of the armchairs. Light pours in from outside through the windows, framed by floor to ceiling curtains.

Exposed dark wood beams overhead lead my eye to the flatscreen TV mounted on the wall opposite the couch, and I hide a smile. Okay, a little bit of a bachelor, then.

"Here we go." Tag sits next to me carefully, holding a big blue mug of steaming hot chocolate in each hand. I grab coasters for him to set them both on the coffee table. "Careful," he warns. "The mugs are hot, too."

I brush my fingertips along the ceramic and yelp. "It'll warm me up, though."

"No, here. I'll help you," Tag offers, pulling my hands into his again and cupping them gently. "And you won't even get burned."

I can't quite breathe for a moment. Every time Tag touches me, my world flips upside down and my whole world seems to point to him. My gaze flicks up to his face. "Promise?" I whisper.

His Adam's apple bobs. He's slow to meet my look. When he finally does, there's that familiar wall—the part of him that he doesn't want me to see.

I wish I could figure him out. He's so generous, welcoming me to his time and life. Yet he's holding back, too, like he isn't quite ready for all the promises I want to make.

It *has* only been a week, but time doesn't matter. The moment I saw him, I knew he was the one. Time simply gives you more memories to share.

I want this to work, and I'm ready to let go of all my fears. I might have been more shy at the beginning, but now I'm the one pushing him. I just hope he's ready to be pushed.

"Yeah," Tag murmurs after a moment, like he missed the meaning that we both know perfectly well he understood. Then he stops rubbing my hands and leans forward to wrap his palms around the mug.

I don't like the silence between us, so I wait for him to put down the mug again and then stick my toes against his bare feet.

That lightens the mood. "Hey!" Tag yelps, playing a kind of reverse footsie where I scramble into his lap to pursue his feet as he tries to keep them away from me.

More importantly, it gets me into his lap. The blood stirs from head to toe as I shift my weight, swinging my other knee over his leg to catch my balance. "Hi there yourself."

Tag beams at me. "Well, look at this. I've got a lapful of cutie, and he isn't going to slobber on me."

"Tsch." I click my tongue. "Now, I never promised *that*. In fact, I had every intention to the contrary."

Tag narrows his eyes like he's hopeful that I mean what he thinks. "Huh?"

I bite my lip and widen my eyes, flicking my lashes as I look him up and down. The insides of my thighs tingle where they make contact with his lap. My hands are resting on his broad shoulders, but I let them slip down to his chest.

"*Oh*," Tag whispers, his voice strained. His hands slowly rise to my waist. "I think we're on the same page."

"I've been daydreaming about you for days." I love having Tag here, pinned down under me, even though I know he could effortlessly flip me over if he wanted to. He stays perfectly still, letting me explore his chest with my fingertips.

I sweep my palms around the ripples of his pecs and abs without any particular goal—at least, until my thumbs catch his nipples.

Tag grunts and squeezes his eyes closed, his lips falling open as he trembles under me.

"You like that?" I whisper. I love finding out what makes him tick. It's not just about getting him naked; I'm going take my time to explore every inch of his body.

This time, I take more care to circle my thumbs around the nubs of his nipples that poke through his tight, black shirt.

"*Yes*," Tag manages. His nails dig into my waist, like he wants to pull me against him and grind into me.

I wonder if I can torment him into doing it. A grin spreads across my face, and I slide my hands down to his waist before making my way under his shirt.

His bare skin against my palms is a delightful feast. Hot, smooth, and perfect.

"Cold," Tag mumbles, but he's not pushing me away or protesting. His voice is a breathy moan, and the bulge in his pants is bigger than ever. I lick my lips, resisting the temptation to scoot closer and push my aching cock against his.

I catch my breath, pushing the fabric up his belly with my fingers. "But good?"

"Very," Tag whispers. "We'll see if I—*agh!*"

I've found his nipples. Two of my fingertips brush against one nipple and then the other, making him arch off the couch as a strangled cry falls from his lips.

Oh, fuck, that's hot.

"If you like it now?" I innocently whisper. "I take it that's a yes."

Tag mumbles something that sounds like a swear word, his head tipped back to bare his throat. Every muscle in his body trembles and pulls tight.

I grin and pinch the nubs carefully between my fingertips, experimentally rolling them. Everything I do seems to turn Tag on, which turns me on. His shirt keeps getting in the way, though.

"Get this off," I mumble, fumbling with the hem. Tag chuckles and raises his arms to help me yank it off, all the way up his strong arms to his wrists. Then he throws it aside and sprawls under me again, shirtless and *gorgeous*.

He's looking at me again with those deep, soulful eyes. "You like what you see?"

I nod so hard that Tag snorts with laughter. Then I spread my knees and wiggle backward on his lap a little so that I can bend over and kiss him.

Oh, God, it's incredible. I know he's snuck a taste of the hot chocolate because I can taste it on his mouth, a sweet burst across my tongue. His lips are soft and warm, and utterly addictive.

I'm tingling from head to toe by the time I pull away to catch my breath. My world spins as heat burns straight to the tips of my toes. I won't be cold for much longer.

"I've never sucked a cock before, but I've always wanted to." The words leave my mouth before I even think about them. But I'm too turned on to be embarrassed.

"Do you want me to show you how it's done?" Tag's voice rumbles, low and sexy, and I might just die of arousal. "For what it's worth, I'm tested and negative. And I assume…"

I chuckle sheepishly. "Yeah, you're the first guy I've been with. So I assume that's fine."

"Mmhmm. Sexy little virgin," Tag murmurs, his eyes focused

and hungry. "I like sucking dick without a condom. What do you say?"

My whole body surges with a fresh wave of pleasure, my aching cock pressing against the front of my damp jeans. Why did I wear jeans for a snow date, anyway? I know better.

"Yes," I gasp. "If you get me out of these wet clothes, you can do anything you want."

Tag chuckles. "An offer I can't resist." He yanks my sweater and shirt off at the same time, hauling all the fabric up and over my head without hesitation.

I catch his shoulders for balance when my torso is laid bare, but Tag isn't wasting time. His warm fingertips trail over my belly until I giggle and squirm with the burst of ticklish sensation that strikes me. Then he yanks open the button and slides down the zipper on my jeans.

I brace myself on his shoulders as I stand up, wriggling while he hauls the denim down and off.

"Oh, God, that feels better," I groan, kicking them off at last. The warm air from the fireplace touches my bare skin. Heat settles into me from the outside as well as the inside: I'm burning up with need for him.

I'm still in my underwear, but I don't know for how much longer. Tag pulls me to sit down next to him, and then he slithers to the floor on his knees in front of me.

"Oh," I squeak, quivering from head to toe. Holy *fuck*. I've imagined this every night since my daring office exploits, but it's so much better in real life.

Just gazing down the length of my body at Tag makes me swell in my underwear, my whole body tightening.

Tag's gaze flicks up and down my body, lingering on the distinctive line of my shaft. "Fuck, you're hot."

"Please," I whisper. I don't know what he's planning, but I'm going to go crazy if he teases me and draws it out.

Tag smiles, warm and genuine and caring. His hand gently runs up the outside of my thigh and over my hip, and then his fingers close around my nipple and do something that makes my whole body surge to life with a lightning strike.

"Fuuuck!" I whimper, arching off the couch.

Tag takes advantage, and his thumbs slip into the waistband of my underwear. He yanks them down and off, lifting one of my feet out. Then he slips between my thighs again, leaving me to kick them off the other ankle.

He's busy kissing a trail up from the inside of my knee, igniting nerves I had no idea existed. My cock is flat against my stomach now, flushed and hard and begging for attention.

The tip of his tongue trails up my thigh as heat pulsates through me, insistent and raw. I gasp for breath, grabbing the back of the couch cushions.

Then Tag stops, his lips on the hollow of the inside of my thigh. Just inches away from my shaft, where all the heat in my body seems to pool. I need him, *need him* so badly he doesn't understand.

"You like that?" Tag murmurs.

All I can manage is a strangled cry, half protest and half plea. Even his knowing chuckle makes my toes curl into the floor.

"All right. I was going to take my time and lick every inch of you. Your nipples..." Tag's hand rises, his fingertips flicking quickly across one of them, making my body draw tight with a sudden flush of heat. "Your belly... your lips..."

"*No,*" I grunt with all my might. "*Now.*" I manage to crack my eyes open and gaze down at him again, glaring.

Tag grins and finally takes mercy. He brushes the backs of his fingers along my shaft, and it jumps under his touch. He chuckles again, curling his hand around it.

At last, the desperation settles into a steady flush of manageable heat. I can try to make this last.

But then he leans in, wrapping his hot lips around the head, and wet heat engulfs me. I whimper again, choking out my ecstasy while the tip of his tongue circles around my sensitive skin.

This is going to be embarrassingly quick. It's a hundred times better than I'd daydreamed.

I can't stop staring as he wraps his sensual lips around me and takes me into his mouth. The soft heat of his tongue flickers along the underside of my shaft, and then the head of my cock slips into his tight throat.

Holy shit, this is amazing.

As I whimper and quiver under his hands, Tag's gaze flickers up to me. Then he sucks in his cheeks, and suddenly the heat around me is unbearably tight in the best way possible.

Tag pulls back until his mouth engulfs just the tip of my cock. Then he curls his fingers around the base of my shaft and bobs his head again until his lips touch his fingers.

Every inch of me is squeezing tight as I gasp raggedly for breath. "Yes," I manage at last. "*More.*"

He knows exactly what I mean. He bobs his head quickly, gulping my cock over and over in a quick, relentless rhythm. The wet sounds and the vibrations of pleasure through every nerve as his lips drag across the velvety skin of my shaft... that would be almost enough to send me over the edge.

But the sight is what really does it. His cheeks are flushed, his gaze focused so tenderly on my cock like it's the tastiest thing he's ever known.

I stare hungrily down at him. I've entrusted him with my pleasure, but this is more than pleasure. It's ecstasy, and I can't stop it. I should try to draw it out, but I'm losing control.

My hips rise as my whole body draws tight, and I try to choke out a warning. I scrabble at his shoulders frantically. But Tag doesn't heed me. He just swallows me to the back of his throat, his other hand running up my front to play with my nipples again.

He wants to swallow. Oh, God!

That realization propels me over the edge hard and fast until I'm flailing in midair. I buck uncontrollably, every muscle going tight at once.

Heat floods through my shaft, spilling into Tag's mouth. I can't look away as he takes my load, sucking his mouth tight around the head of my shaft. The wet noises as he swallows and laps at my slit for more are so fucking hot.

I whimper, scrabbling at his shoulders as he wrings out every droplet of pleasure before I finally start to go limp. I sprawl helplessly on the couch, my muscles utterly wrung out.

Tag finally pulls away and wipes his mouth. "Thank you for bringing dessert."

I raise my hands to my face as I giggle so hard I can't breathe. He's ridiculous, and it should sound corny, but it's strangely hot at the same time. Maybe it's the boldness with which he says it.

"Your turn?" I whisper. "It might take me a minute to… function…" I can't imagine having any kind of coordination right now.

Tag just smiles and shakes his head as he rises to sit next to me on the couch. "Next time," he promises. "Now you know how it's done."

"I don't know if I do," I laugh, curling into him and pulling my knees up so I can wriggle into his lap again. I fling my arms around his shoulders and bury my nose in his neck. "But thank you."

"Oh, it was my pleasure," Tag chuckles softly. His arms snake around me, and I relax into his strong hold.

I can't imagine a more perfect snow day, or a more perfect man to share it with. Whatever lies in store for us, it's worth it just to catch a glimpse of the devotion on Tag's face.

It's one thing to hear him tell me how he feels, but it's another to see it for myself and feel it in every gentle caress and tender moment of intimacy. I'm ready for a future filled with these moments.

Meeting my family tomorrow doesn't seem so scary anymore. Nor does the poetry night. I can do anything with Tag by my side.

20

TAG

"So how long ago did you move here? Pass the potatoes, please?"

I quickly grab the bowl of mashed potatoes and set it in front of… my brain flails for a moment before her name comes to me: Lily. She's married to Elijah, the oldest brother and the lawyer.

It's a lot of people to meet all at once, but I've memorized all their names and faces. It's weird to be using all the skills I developed in meet-and-greets while desperately hiding the source of that very talent.

Caleb's parents and all three of his older brothers are there, along with their wives. Of course they're all happy newlyweds. Poor Caleb must feel adrift as the only single one here.

Well, sorta-kinda-single now. We haven't talked about labels yet, but I hope we will… as long as I pass this test with flying colors. I'm doing everything I can to impress them, from my best table manners to all the small talk about goings-on in Burlington.

"Four years," I tell Lily as I pick up my fork again. "Bought a farmhouse out here."

"Yeah, the place up by the creek? Lily and I looked at that," Eli interjects. "Looked like it needed work."

I laugh and groan theatrically. "You bet it did. Totally worth it, though. It was such a beautiful old place."

"It looks really nice now," Caleb meekly interjects.

"Thanks." I glance across the table at him with a little smile. I'm glad to hear him say anything at all. He's been very quiet so far tonight. Is this how he always is around them, or is it because I'm here?

Caleb smiles briefly and then looks at his plate again. I wish he were sitting next to me so I could squeeze his hand reassuringly. *See?* I want to tell him. *It's all going fine.*

"And you run that winery, Silver Crown? How's that going?" Caleb's father, Luke, asks.

Meadery, I want to correct him, but this isn't the moment. I told them I'm a winemaker so I don't have to explain how honey ferments for the thousandth time.

Caleb's dad seems easygoing, but I know why he's asking. He's trying to figure out if I'm a successful business owner or a madman with a couple of beehives, a crazy plan, and a bunch of debt.

The rest of the family is all watching me, too. It's way worse than being on any stage. But I try to calm down and reassure myself that people understand a few mistakes in a performance as long as you entertain them.

I can do that tonight—I just have to figure out the right balance between making fun of myself and presenting myself as a serious candidate for Caleb's affections.

"Really well," I tell him with a smile. "I never thought I'd love it so much, but I do. Sales have been going up every quarter for the last couple of years."

"That's wonderful to hear," Caleb's mom—Michelle—tells me, and his dad nods approvingly.

"Yeah. Takes time for people to hear about it and try it, and then they get hooked and tell their friends… it's a slow game, but I'm patient. Takes time to get things right."

I deliberately look across the table at Caleb with those last words, a smile touching my lips.

Caleb blushes and meets my gaze like he's thinking the same thing. *Not that we took much time.*

"But when the right thing comes along, you just know," Lee says with a lilt to his voice that I'm certain is teasing.

The glare Caleb shoots him is only confirmation.

I politely smile and nod, then redirect the conversation to their careers, but it only lasts long enough to let me finish my roast ham and potatoes. By the time dessert is served, I'm in the spotlight once more.

"So, about your intentions with my little brother..." That's Lee, grinning like the Cheshire Cat while his wife, Sarah, jabs him with an elbow.

I chuckle, trying to sound more confident than I feel. I've prepared an answer, but I didn't even have to think about it. It's the truth. "Whatever Caleb wants, Caleb gets."

"Just like the rest of his life," Eli shakes his head mock-seriously. "Our spoiled baby brother."

"Hey. Whatever I got, you guys arm-wrestled me for. Or negotiated over. I earned it all fair and square." Caleb's cheeks are bright red, but he's trying to stand up for himself at least, and that makes me happy.

"Hey, are you brothers?" I feign surprise and set down my fork. "Wow."

"I know. It's so hard to tell. Sometimes it seems like we get along," Kelvin says.

"Well, he doesn't seem like a weirdo or an online dating scammer, so my vote is yes," Lee says with a grin at me. "But only since you like him, little brother. No, no, I'm kidding," he raises his hand before his wife can elbow him again. "I just thought you might be too good to be true. But hey. Anyone offering to take him off our hands at last..."

I swallow hard. I can't ride the wave of his incessant joking when he hits too close to home. I'm not out to hurt Caleb, and I'm definitely not a catfish. But... I kind of am.

"*Lee,*" Michelle scolds her son as she folds her napkin, but the others laugh. She looks over at me with a warm smile. "You're more than welcome to our table and our family."

"Thank you," I tell her, and I manage a smile. Then I quickly compliment her on the apple pie and dig in, so I don't have to say anything.

I'm hardly hungry, though. The nerves might have settled, but the guilt has replaced that weight in my stomach.

They're all being so nice—maybe a little hard-assed, but nice nonetheless. Despite my fears, none of them have recognized me or asked me questions that forced me to lie.

Not-lying isn't the truth, though. I'm only telling Caleb half the story.

I've got excuses for days.

It's only been a week, after all, and I don't just tell everyone I know. I don't want Caleb's family to blow my hard-won anonymity. I don't want them assuming I'm some egotistic rich guy. I can't tell Caleb the rest of the story right now for the first time in front of his whole family.

Excuses coming out of my ass.

I also don't want to tell Caleb tonight, or tomorrow, or… *ever*. I want to just pretend that guy doesn't exist anymore, that I've always been this one.

But that's unrealistic. My parents are going to want to meet Caleb when they next visit. They usually remember to call me Tag now, but no way can I ask them to keep my secrets.

Or before then, someone with a good memory for faces will spot me and it'll all be over. I'm surprised it hasn't happened in the last four years, but I've also kept to myself for most of that time.

The family's conversation is back to the deck outside, which gives me a great reason to say nothing and let them argue out dimensions and types of lumber.

I have to tell him soon. Crap.

I hate that idea. I hate giving him a chance to think less of me for selling my soul to the machine, and I hate admitting what happened to me.

It wasn't just my choice to leave. But the way I got kicked out? Downright humiliating. It made the news, the founding singer of the up-and-coming rock band of the decade being kicked out on stage in a live, intimate concert.

It was as much a surprise for me as the fans that night. I did the professional thing—unlike those assholes—and went along with it. Pretended like I had a say in it, because I knew damn well the lawyers would find a way to screw me over if I didn't.

But as much as it scares and embarrasses me, how much worse can it be than Caleb bringing me to meet his family or facing down his stage fright? It's not like I can take this secret to my deathbed.

The only way to assuage my guilt is to promise myself that this is just the first meeting. The trial run. The next time I see Caleb's family, I'll come clean about everything.

That means telling Caleb first, and if I don't put a deadline on it now… I think I never will, until it's too late.

"Tomorrow night." Caleb's words shake me out of my reverie and I blink at him, looking around like I didn't just tune the fuck out. "Bees and Beats," he adds with a wink at me. "Not my name."

I grin sheepishly and raise my hand. "Guilty. I'm awful at naming things."

"It sounds fun, though. And we've got to try more." Lily points at the empty mead bottles on the table. I brought two, but they were gone in a flash with compliments all around. "We'll get Leanne to look after the kids again?" she asks Eli, who nods.

Oh, God. Within moments, every person around the table promises to show up tomorrow. This time, instead of Caleb being nervous, he's proud and excited and I'm shitting a brick.

Tomorrow night.

That's when I'll tell Caleb, after the poetry reading. When I've shown him that I can pull out all the stops to support him, and

I've shared the work that truly comes from my heart instead of the bland stuff everyone's heard on the radio.

When he sees for certain that the whole rock star persona is gone, and I'm just Tag now. The guy who loves him and wants to give him everything he's ever dreamed of.

I'll prove how I feel about Caleb first, and then I'll tell him the good, the bad, and the downright ugly. In the meantime, I'll just pray that I don't scare him off forever.

CALEB

"I think that went great."

I'm a little bit tipsy, so I'm glad Tag is doing the driving again. I could get used to being ferried around in his white pickup truck. It's not a pumpkin carriage, but it feels pretty damn close.

We're heading to his place now so I can practice my performance. I think it'll be more flirting than practice, but that's A-OK with me. I *should* try to pick up more anti-stage fright tips, but I'm too giggly and high from the relief of how well dinner went.

I roll my head to the side and gaze at the man, trying to find words for my admiration. He handled everyone so brilliantly tonight, from Eli's scrutiny to Lee's merciless teasing.

I'd like to think I'm pretty straightforward, but my family is a handful. And if Tag can handle them, he can handle anything.

"Mmhmm," Tag murmurs, his eyes on the road. He throws on his turn signal as he pulls out of the little suburban street where my parents live, heading for his place.

"You're not scarred for life?" I reach across the seat to poke his thigh gently.

"Nuh-uh."

"Give it time. Once they get dirt on you, they'll never let it go." I giggle, he smiles, and I relax.

I'm glad he likes my laughter. It always seems to make him smile. He doesn't get uptight about me not being the manliest man on the planet. Same with my lisp—it's stronger when I've been drinking.

Everything I used to think would scare off a big, strong guy like him just seems to enchant him.

And I'm just as smitten with everything Tag says and does. I'm so happy that I get to spend another night with him. The world seems like a better place all of a sudden.

"I might treat you tonight," Tag says suddenly as he stops at a red light.

I bite my lip as a prickle of heat works its way through me. "Mmhmm?" I try for my most seductive response.

Tag laughs. "Oh, no. I've corrupted your sweet, innocent mind."

"Corrupted me, sure. My mind was never sweet or innocent, though." I conspiratorially hold a finger to my lips. "Don't tell anyone."

"Jesus." Tag rests a hand on his head for a moment, and then lays it on the seat between us. He actually looks guilty as the light changes and he pulls away. "I didn't realize you were *that* much of a lightweight."

I pout at him and put my hand in his. I wish I'd slid into the middle seat instead of this one. The truck is huge and it feels like we're a mile apart. "Don't worry, I'm not *that* drunk. Just high on life. On… you."

I can't find a better way to express the fact that every time he speaks, a choir of angels seems to point to him and tell me, *That one. Hold on to him.*

Yeah, I plan to.

"Oh." Tag can't hide his smile. "Okay."

I smile all the way back to his place, and once he's parked and he sticks his head in to check on Queenie, the two of us head out to the tasting room.

"We could do it in the house, but it feels more like a bar in here. Plus, we're alone."

"I'll do it anywhere with you," I giggle as I squirm against him, shivering cold. I knew I'd be getting straight into the truck so I didn't wear my jacket today, and it's getting freaking cold out at night. "Alone or not."

"Jesus, Caleb. You're going to distract me if you're not careful." Tag slips his key into the lock and turns it, then pushes the door open and holds it for me.

I wink. "Good." Then I make a show of grinding past him in order to step through the doorway, ignoring his groan.

But despite my wild fantasies, he doesn't grab me and fling me to the floor to go to town.

Not yet, anyway. We've got time.

"You brought your poetry?" Tag asks, flicking the lights on. Then he closes and locks the door behind us. Damn it, he really does want to practice. At least I won't be self-conscious if it's just him here.

"I did." The folded pages are shoved into my back pocket. I've been squirming on them all evening at supper, but I didn't want to put them on the table in case I forgot them—or Lee decided to do a dramatic reading.

Tag sinks onto the chair at one of the tables. "All right. Find somewhere comfortable to stand."

I frown and look around. "It's not going to be the same without a stage." My eyes land on the bar top, but before I can say a word, Tag grabs my arm.

"Not a chance." He actually seems genuinely worried, which is really sweet.

I grin at him. "What's the worst that could happen?"

"Bodily harm," Tag nods. "Full body cast. Try performing in one of those."

"That's okay, you can hold my pages and turn them for me."

His eyes light up with amusement. "May I? Thank you."

"As long as you stay out of my spotlight."

Tag tips his head back and laughs richly, his eyes sparkling as he shakes his head slightly. The fondness on his face makes me glow with pride. *I* did that. I made him happy.

"Oh, I..." Tag says, and then he abruptly stops. His eyes go a little bit wide. Then he quickly carries on. "I really like you."

Fuck. I think he nearly said it. And he's not the only one.

It may be fast, but does that really matter? We're both adults, even if I'm not very experienced. We each know what we want. Why drag it out with doubts and second-guessing? I'd rather lock that shit down.

I already know Tag is everything I'm looking for in a guy. Total dreamboat. And it makes me ridiculously happy that he nearly slipped up and said it—the L-word. I'm sure of it.

"I 'really like' you too," I say with a huge, silly grin that I can't stop. I might be teasing him just a little bit. Then I pretend to cough. "But I can't read with such a dry throat."

Tag leaps to his feet and strides for the bar as I beam at his retreating back. "What can I get you? No, wait. I have an idea. I can make you something. A surprise."

I lean my hip against the nearest table as I unfold and flatten out the pages, smiling to myself. "Is that the surprise you promised me?"

"Huh? Oh, no. That's something else."

"Oooh." I shiver with happiness this time. "You spoil me."

"Not nearly as much as I want to," Tag assures me.

I blush, biting my lip and watch him focusing on pouring things into a cocktail shaker. I have no idea what he's making me, but I'm okay with that. He knows what I like, and I trust him to choose something good.

"Hold on, I need something," Tag mumbles and hurries out of the tasting room while I laugh.

"What on earth..."

When he returns, awkwardly opening the door with his shoulder, he's got a brown egg in each hand. "Farm fresh," he says, holding them up with a big, winning smile.

I can't stop my laughter, but I'm completely enchanted. He could have just blended mead with some soda or something, but he's going the whole nine yards.

"Egg white? Or are you skipping ahead to breakfast?"

"Nothing says this can't be breakfast," Tag waggles his brows as I giggle again.

"Mmm. Good point. Now I know what to order with my toast and poached eggs."

After a little more shaking and stirring and pouring and stealthy tasting that I pretend not to notice, Tag emerges from behind the counter with two tall, elegantly curved glasses.

I catch my breath at the elegant presentation. The glasses are filled with some reddish-pink cocktail with foam on top, and he's even put a cherry on the rim of each glass.

"Thank you. What's it called?" I ask, taking the glass and gently clinking it against his for a toast.

Tag catches my gaze and holds it, and suddenly I can't blink or look away. The depth of feeling in his eyes almost hurts. "Hmm… I think…" he murmurs, but I can tell he's already decided. "I think I'll call it The Poet."

I could just about cry. I bite my lip, finally tearing my gaze away from his so that I can carefully sip.

Oh, God, it's incredible. Cherry and almond wash over my tongue first, followed by a bite of… lemon? It's foamy and playful and perfect.

Tag is sipping from his own glass, watching me anxiously for my verdict.

"I love it," I murmur and look straight at him, hoping he knows what I mean: I love *you*.

Tag's cheeks flush. "Good," he murmurs, and I'm not fooled by his steady voice. "Now, how about you practice?" His hand shakes as he sets his glass on the table and clears his throat.

I shake my head. With so many thoughts of Tag running around my head, I don't want to pull away from him and practice performing. That's a problem for tomorrow night. "It's not the same. I can read anything out to you. Being on stage is a different experience."

"Hmm." Tag acknowledges my point with a little nod. "Come here, then."

I scramble onto the chair next to him and set my papers down, swapping them for my cocktail glass. "Plus, I don't want to be parted from this cocktail."

This cocktail. Not *you.* But he knows what I mean. Tag runs his hand down my thigh gently, taking my hand.

"I'm glad you like it. Now, did you want to find out what my surprise is?"

I bite my lip and look him up and down, trying for a comical yet sexy expression. "Oh, yes, *please.*"

Tag cracks up again and leans in for an affectionate kiss. "Okay. I don't do this for just anyone. In fact… I haven't done it in a long time."

There are so many inappropriate jokes that I can't choose just one. By the time I push them all to the side, Tag has stood up and taken down the guitar from the wall.

"You're kidding. You play?" I gasp. I thought it was just ornamental. This is insane. My life is a movie. He's made me a custom cocktail and he's about to serenade me with a guitar. I'm literally melting into happy goo.

"Don't judge me if I screw up. Literally, it's been years."

I shake my head. I doubt I'd notice anyway, but it doesn't matter. He could be the worst guitar player in the world and the pants would still magically melt off me.

But he's not the worst. In fact, he's really good. So good that I almost forget to drink my cocktail because my jaw is hanging open.

His fingers dance along the chords like he was born to it, and he hums a little bit here and there. The melody flowing from his fingers is soft but filled with meaning.

I can't stop staring. "Jesus," I whisper when the last note finally fades. "You're talented."

Where the hell did he learn to play so well? Who was he, before he became a beekeeper in the woods?

Tag flushes a little bit and doesn't look at me. "Thanks," he mumbles, biting his lip. Despite my praise, he looks nervous as all hell. He must be as shy about his music as I am about my poetry.

"No, really." I shake my head in awe. "Wow."

Tag clears his throat and stands up, hanging up the guitar carefully. He looks like he's holding something back—something he can't quite dare to say.

Or ask. And I think I know what it is. Luckily for him, I've already made up my mind.

There's so much I don't know about him, but I don't need to. He's the perfect catch, and I'm not going to let him slip away.

"Tag," I whisper and pull him to sit down next to me again. I keep a hold on his hand. "I really like the time we've spent together. I know it hasn't been long, but it feels like it."

"Yeah," he agrees, his eyes soft and warm. He leans in to brush his lips against mine.

Even that distractingly slow, beautiful kiss doesn't stop me. The moment he pulls away, I cup the back of his head with a trembling hand.

I have to try. There's no better moment.

"If you asked me out... I wouldn't say no." I grin at him despite my nerves.

"You mean..." A slow smile grows on Tag's lips. "Wait, are you trying to..."

I gulp hard. "I want you to be my boyfriend," I whisper. "Would you go out with me? Like, make this official?"

"Oh my God." Tag looks surprised more than anything, but not in a bad way. He's just looking at me like he's not sure I know what I'm signing up for.

But hell, yeah, I do. A multitalented boyfriend who believes in me? He's a dream come true.

"Caleb, I…" He scratches his head, and then he takes my shoulder. "I… Wow. I was waiting until… but that was out of the blue. God, you don't stop surprising me," he chuckles. He takes a breath and lets it out, like he's making up his mind and composing himself at last. "I'd be crazy to say no. I like you, too. A lot. So… yeah. I'd love to go out with you."

"Boyfriends?" I squeak.

He chuckles softly and cups the back of my head, hauling me in for a kiss. "Boyfriends," he murmurs against my lips.

I pull back and squeal, vibrating in my seat. He laughs, but the scream of excitement is impossible to stop.

"You said yes!"

His eyes sparkle. "I'm pretty sure I did, yeah."

I lunge at him, nearly knocking his chair over, and fling my arms around him.

Tag's beautiful laugh fills the room as he catches me and hugs me tightly. "Hello, my gorgeous boyfriend," he murmurs, and I can just about die happy.

He's really into me. Really *really*, like… for real. So I can't let him down. I'm going to do my best to show him that I'm talented and hardworking and going places.

I foresee not much lunch happening on my lunch break tomorrow. I'm going to take my poetry to the bathroom at work and practice reading it. Anything to make tomorrow go well.

But first, I have a favor to return.

I grin and wriggle free from his hold at last, bracing my hands on the arms of his chair. "I think we should celebrate this."

"What did you have in mind?"

I run my hands up Tag's arms to his shoulders, biting my lower lip. "Well, since you were such a good teacher, it's my turn to play student."

"Of…" Tag starts to say before he trails off. His eyebrows shoot to his hairline as his lips part. He breathes a soft *Oh* of realization.

I smirk and bend over to press my lips against his shirt, right above his abs. My fingers walk down his sides to his strong thighs, and then I rub all the way to his knees and back up again.

I love the thought of pleasing him right here.

"*Caleb*," Tag groans. "Jesus. I'm sure this technically breaks a license, but I don't care."

"That's the spirit," I beam up at him. I brace myself on his legs as I push them apart and crowd up to him. Then I bend over so I can kiss his thighs. It's a bit awkward at this height, but I don't want to stop and make him move to the bench behind me.

One hand runs along my back. He's obviously noticed the same thing. "Are you going to be okay with—"

It's sweet of him to worry, but I interrupt his concern by catching the zipper of his jeans in his teeth and hauling it down. "With?" I flutter my lashes.

"*Fuck*," Tag strangles out as a tent grows in front of my eyes.

"Oh, I'd love to fuck," I retort with a mischievous grin. "But I owe you this first."

"You don't… owe me…" Tag tries to tell me, but I've slipped my fingers in through his fly and I'm caressing his rapidly hardening shaft. "Oh my God," he groans, grabbing my shoulders. "Caleb!"

I love the stinging little lines that dig into my skin as he loses his self-control. His breath comes fast and loud now, especially when I dig the heel of my palm against his shaft and drag it up to the tip.

Then I yank down his jeans and underwear, wasting no time going for what I want. His hard cock bobs free, poking straight up in the air in front of my face. It's flushed pink, the head round and beautiful. There's already a drop of moisture at the slit that makes me lick my lips.

"Yes," Tag growls, and just like I'd hoped, his fingers rise to my hair. He's gentle—too gentle.

I reach up to lay my hand on his, then clench my fingers tightly around his. "Hold on tight," I grin up at him. "It's going to be a wild ride."

Tag twists his fingers around my hair and pulls lightly, and a rainfall of sparks prickle along my scalp. I whimper with delight, bowing my neck to lap at the head of his dick.

The first thing I do is lick off the wet droplet of precum. It's a hint of delicious Tag right here against my tongue. The taste is strange but wonderful—not spicy, bitter, or sweet, but something all of its own.

I'll have to do my taste testing later. Tag's strangled groan and the twitch of his shaft in front of my eyes tells me that he's desperate for me.

And God, that makes a guy's ego grow.

His shaft is velvety and warm to the touch, but rock hard, too. I gently tweak it, pulling it toward me and letting it spring up a few times as he moans in pleasure.

Then I wrap my fingers around him, gently tugging them from base to tip and pushing back down again. And I lean down to suck the head of his cock into my mouth.

It's incredible. I love the heat on my tongue and the strangled noises he makes as I awkwardly close my lips around him. It takes a bit of work to keep my lips between him and my teeth, but it's not like I haven't practiced over the last three days.

Sure, I got a few weird looks at the grocery store for buying Popsicles in winter, but now? Totally worth it.

He throbs under my tongue, the heat and weight of him utterly addictive. I swirl my tongue around the head and lick the shaft before closing my lips around the tip.

Everything I try, Tag rewards with a sound—sometimes soft, other times harsh and loud. It doesn't take long to figure out how to wrap my fingers around the thick base of his shaft and hold him steady so I can bob my head, swallowing him deeper into my mouth.

More droplets of precum trickle down my tongue and throat, sharp and musky and delicious. I'm greedy for more. I want to feel him fuck my mouth until he lets go.

He swallowed, so I will, too. I want to make him feel amazing. *Need* to.

"God, Caleb," Tag whispers, his voice hoarse. "You're incredible. That feels so good."

"Mmm?" I hum around his shaft, making him vibrate a little and giggling at the sharp grunt he gives in reaction. I hum again, long and low, so he can feel it straight to the core.

Then I hold my head still and hunch over a little more, softening and bending my knees. It's a lot of work, but I find the right angle at last. I'm staring up his body and just about making eye contact.

And he's *hungry*. "Yes," my brand-new boyfriend grunts. His nails dig into my scalp as he closes his fist around my hair, thrusting up into my mouth.

I whimper and hold still, relishing the drag of sensitive skin against my lips and the gentleness he's trying so hard to keep in his movements.

That won't last long, I hope.

Sure enough, within a minute his hips are flexing fast and hard as he stares down at the sight.

"That's… the sexiest thing I've seen in my life," Tag whispers. "I wish you could see what it looks like."

I raise a brow, but he doesn't let me pull my mouth away to make a suggestion. So I clumsily point my thumb to my ear, pinky to my jaw. *Phone.*

"You dirty man," Tag chuckles deeply, fumbling in his jeans. He manages to get the phone out of his pocket, and I squirm with delight as the light suddenly flashes on.

Oh, my God, he's recording.

I suddenly surge into action, gripping the base of his cock and sucking him deep into my mouth, rough and hungry. I bob my head hard and fast as soft grunts slide from me.

"Keep that up and I'm gonna come," Tag warns me, his voice gritty. "I'm so fucking close."

I whimper my approval. *Good. Let me swallow your load, please.*

"You gonna swallow like a good boyfriend?" Tag whispers and lets go of my hair, caressing my cheek. It's fond, yet dominant and so freaking hot. I squirm again, heat shooting straight to my hard dick. "Gonna take my whole load and suck me dry?"

I peek up toward his face—and the phone camera, which only makes me hotter—and manage to grunt a quiet *Mmhmm* around his shaft. I can feel it too, his shaft swelling in my mouth and the way he catches his breath.

I already want to see this replay, and it's not even over yet!

Tag's eyes slide closed, and for a single, perfect moment, he's frozen. His whole body tightens and arches... and then he cries out in a rough gasp. His sticky mess fills my mouth and it's all I can do to swallow it in big, hasty gulps. It's thick and sticky, coating my tongue completely.

And I love it. I haven't even put a finger on myself, but I'm so turned on I could burst. So happy.

When his desperate little movements stop and I suck the last few droplets clean, I straighten up, shove my hands in my pants, and pull myself out.

Tag was shifting like he was about to turn off the camera, but he stops and stares over his phone instead, his hands sinking a little bit in the air like he can't quite believe it.

I grin and brace myself on his shoulder, wrapping my hand around myself. Then I start stroking myself. I'm showing off a little for the camera, twisting my wrist at the end of each stroke, letting my lashes flutter closed as I bite my lip.

"Tag," I breathe as my hand flies along my shaft. "I'm gonna... I can't stop it!"

"Come for me, baby," Tag whispers. "My beautiful boyfriend. Show me what you've got."

I grin, hardly able to tear my eyes away from him... but I can't help it. I throw my head back, baring my throat and clutching the back of his chair for dear life. "Yes!" My cry rings through the room as blackness slams into me.

My knees buckle, and Tag's arm slides around my waist as I

collapse onto him in a heap. For the second time tonight, I thank Tag mentally for buying solid furniture.

"So gorgeous," Tag whispers, his warm lips finding my ear and neck. He hoists me up a little more and kisses my lips, and I giggle softly. He doesn't seem to mind tasting himself. "That was amazing. Thank you."

"No," I mumble and kiss his shoulder. "Thank *you* for documenting it."

Tag grins at me. "I'll send it to you. We can watch it together on nights we're apart."

Then I pout. "Apart?" I tease. "You're killing the mood."

I'm not completely joking, either. I don't want to think about spending another night that isn't in his arms.

"Shh," Tag soothes me and hastily kisses my cheek. "Come to bed with me."

"Much better."

He grabs his phone and my hand, towing me out of the meadery, locking up, and straight to the house. I'm so tired that by the time we get inside and all the way to the top of the stairs, I'm just about ready to faceplant into bed.

So I do, only reluctantly squirming around to kick all the rest of my clothes off.

When we're both naked and the light is out, Tag pulls back the covers and helps me squirm underneath. I roll over with my back to him, he puts his arm around me, and I crack my lashes for just long enough to admire the beam of moonlight across the floor.

Yes. This is perfect.

Tag holds onto me really tight tonight. A little more so than before. Is he full of feelings, or is he nervous? He feels nervous. His breathing is short, and he's fidgety.

He doesn't have to be nervous. His guitar is good. Even if his poetry sucks, I'll still love him. I don't think there's anything he could do to make me stop loving him.

Nothing short of feeding me to his bees, anyway.

I stifle a giggle, but when Tag makes a questioning noise, I giggle again and shake my head. "Good night."

He chuckles and shakes his head, then presses a kiss against the curls at the back of my head. "Good night, Caleb."

It doesn't matter what tomorrow brings: we'll get through it together.

22

TAG

"Ding dong," I call out as I knock on the door at the top of Caleb's stairs.

He's laughing as he pulls it open. "If I am, so are you. Hi, babe." Then he tilts his head. "Baby? Honey?"

He's obviously nervous if he's already chattering, and he can't stop twisting his hands together. So I step forward, cup his cheeks gently, and press a kiss against his mouth.

Caleb sighs a warm, contented breath as I seek out his lower lip, gently tugging between my teeth. I flick my tongue until he relaxes and melts in my arms.

"Better?" I ask softly, bumping our noses together before I pull back, still holding his arms.

"Mmhmm." Caleb's eyes flicker open as he gazes at me. "Thank you." He takes a deep breath and lets it out, then tugs on my jacket. "Let me just get my shoes on and stuff. Or is it too soon? It's too soon."

I chuckle and step inside, then pluck at his shirt. "Look at this. My gorgeous poet boyfriend."

"Is it too artsy?" Caleb bites his lip. "I bought it today but I wasn't sure."

He's wearing black jeans and a billowing collared shirt that goes almost to his mid-thighs. It's dark blue with a subtle purple sheen. It makes me want to unbutton him and kiss him all over.

"It's perfect," I promise.

"Thank God. All I ever wear is stuff I could wear in the office," Caleb groans. Then he seizes my zipper and slides it down for a peek at my white shirt.

I grin and raise my brows, striking a modeling pose with a hand behind my head that makes him giggle. "Approved?" I ask.

Caleb bites his lip playfully, pulling open my jacket. Then he nods, gripping both sides and tugging me in to kiss me. "Approved."

"Phew." I snake my arm around his waist and pull him in, pressing a kiss on his lips. "I'd hate to be sent home to change by the boss."

"*I'm* the boss?" Caleb almost squeaks. "You're the organizer."

"Nah, I'm just the stage manager. You're the talent."

My stomach lurches as the fragments of my old life brush at my memory. Oh, God, I'm just as nervous as Caleb, but not for the event. Afterward will be the real test of my mettle.

I don't know how he's going to react, but it's time to do it anyway. If we're going to be boyfriends, Caleb should know. If he lets it slip to the town… well, I don't think he would.

I know Caleb. I trust him. And I shouldn't let him trust me while I'm keeping secrets. So it's time to let my secret out, no matter what happens.

He slips his arm around mine and walks me to the couch. "So how is it going to work tonight?"

"Super casual and spontaneous," I promise Caleb. He gives me a look, and I grin. "Or… super well-planned?"

"Accountants don't like spontaneity."

"What about poets? Excellent poets who are going to kick ass?"

"Accountants *and* poets will reward all compliments later. Keep a running total," Caleb tells me.

I laugh quickly as I formulate a plan. "How about I go onto

stage first, make up some shit on the fly? I'll talk about my meadery sponsoring the event because of how important nature is to the bees, and how your poetry has to do with nature, and probably also brag to everyone that you're my boyfriend."

Caleb's cheeks flush and he bites his lip.

Oh. Right. His whole family is going to be there. "Unless you haven't told them...?" I trail off. I don't have anyone to tell apart from my parents, but I didn't realize that he might want to keep it quiet.

Caleb clears his throat softly. "I've told everyone who will listen, including my barista and the office janitor."

I can't stop the laugh. It's frankly adorable, and he might look sheepish, but he's also not apologizing. "Okay, good. So I'm cleared to brag. Then I'll introduce you, and you can do your thing. When you want a break, just signal me and I'll take over, entertain the crowd a bit, read out some of my stuff."

"You're a pro," Caleb murmurs with admiration.

I flinch again. For a crazy second, I consider telling him—right here and now. But no, that would be stupid, wouldn't it?

Crap. What if he already knows and he doesn't care? Maybe he was just waiting for me to tell him.

Fuck. Why am I being such a chicken about this? I could at least *start* to tell him.

"Yes. I've been on stage before, but not for a long time," I tell him.

Caleb is staring into the distance. "That's why you're so good. I want to learn to be that good, too. So I've prepared two segments, so there's a few minutes' intermission. Making people listen to half an hour of me would be a lot."

I nod, not sure if I'm more relieved that I get to put this off until later or disappointed that it's still hanging over my head. Of course there isn't an easy way out.

I was about to tell him before he asked me out. I couldn't very well keep him hanging in suspense or crush his spirits. And then he distracted me in the best of ways, and the moment passed.

If I'm being honest, I *let* the moment pass. I was afraid that Caleb would realize who I used to be and judge me for it. My heart couldn't handle it if he'd rejected me just moments later.

But Caleb's clearly slipped into performance mode. If I stop him now and explain, I might snap him out of it and freak him out, and… no, that's not fair. I don't want to throw him out of his own groove by talking about my past.

I had plenty of chances to tell him, and I chickened out every time. This is his moment and I'll let him have it first.

"So we're all ready. Let's get there a few minutes early," I suggest after a moment. "Have a drink, relax, meet people. It'll be less scary if you know who's there and it feels like you're surrounded by friends."

"I might be," Caleb giggles. "I bribed most of my coworkers into coming. And my boss, and my family. So at least the place won't be empty."

I squeeze his arm. "Perfect. If you get nervous, just forget about everyone else, choose the person you know that you think would like that poem the most, and go for it."

Caleb flashes me a grin. "I can do that. I'm not going to let anything keep me down." He springs to his feet and grabs my hand, then leans backward like he's trying to pry me up. He's full of energy, nervous but no longer terrified. I like seeing this.

"Jacket first," I remind him with a laugh before I let him haul me straight to Vino and Veritas.

Nothing seems out of the ordinary until we reach the door of the bar. Before I can open it, a guy standing near the building springs to life and cuts us off.

And then he speaks the words that send a nauseating chill straight to the pit of my stomach.

"Titus? Titus Taylor?"

Fuck. Time seems to slow down until every second is a year long. The blood drains from my face and I freeze, not sure what the hell I'm supposed to say or do.

He's still talking, and some distant part of my brain registers his words. "My name is Rod Graves. I finally tracked you down! You're a hard man to find." He points at the little hand-drawn poster I stuck in the window of the bar with Caleb's name and mine. "You're going by Tag? Are you getting back into the biz? Do you need an agent?"

Like a wrecking ball slamming through my life, the memory hits me: Roxy warned me about an enthusiastic young guy trying to sign me.

Fuck. How the hell did he *find* me?

I still haven't said a word, but as I draw a deep breath to try to speak, Caleb's hand slips from mine. He steps back, his brow furrowing as he looks between us.

Shit. I'm getting dizzy now, my heart thundering in my chest.

"I understand Roxanne still represents Jet Slack, but now that you're flying solo… I think you could benefit from independent representation. So I'll be in the audience tonight, and I want to talk to you after the show."

He's still talking a mile a minute, and neither of us can get a word in edgeways.

Caleb finally cuts him off, holding up his hand. "Excuse me?" His voice is muffled with something that sounds like fear. "This is… Tag. Right, Tag?"

That wide-eyed gaze turns to me, and I can't bear to meet it with my own. Can't face the shock and dismay. Instead, I bite my lip and stare at the ground by his feet as my cheeks flush with heat.

"Er…" Rod trails off at last, apparently noticing that things just got really awkward. I shoot him a glare akin to diamond-tipped steel, and he clears his throat and opens the door of the bar. "I'll leave you to it. Think about it, Titus. Tag."

Then he vanishes inside, leaving me alone to deal with the fallout.

"Tag?" Caleb takes another step away from me, and at last I try to meet his eyes. "What was that?"

"I…" My mouth is paper-dry. I shove my hands in my pockets,

like a few bits of lint or my wallet or keys can help explain this. "I can explain."

"You said you've been on stage before," Caleb murmurs, his voice strange and distant.

I nod tightly, trying to swallow the frog in my airway. I'm so fucking mad at myself that it hurts. And mad at this asshole Rod for showing up. It's all crashing down. All I needed was a few more hours, for God's sake!

"Years ago," I mumble, finally looking at him.

Fuck. There's a wall behind Caleb's eyes that I've never seen before. He's looking at me like a stranger, not a lover.

"In my old life," I add. "I used to perform—"

"In Jet Slack? The band? The *world-famous* band?" Caleb manages, enunciating every syllable in a strangled croak of... I don't know if it's anger or shock, but I don't like either possibility.

I wish I could rewind the last hour. Even if it surprised him, I should have been the one to tell Caleb tonight. Or yesterday. Or last week.

I want to make my excuses and defend myself, but I can't deny it. That would *definitely* be a lie.

So I just nod.

A few seconds pass. We're blocking the doorway as a few people try to get in, but no way in hell am I about to ask Caleb to move this conversation out of the way. I barely even notice them, despite their polite throat-clearing.

"Why?" Caleb whispers at last.

God, so many reasons, but as I scrabble at them, they all feel so flimsy. "I didn't want anyone here knowing."

"Including *me*." Caleb steps backward, but I don't think it's for the sake of the other bar patrons.

I follow him, trying to stay close. "Yes, but..." I shake my head and close my eyes, pressing my hand to my face. "Yes, but only at first. I was going to tell you tonight after the show." Steps scuff on the concrete, and I quickly drop my hand and open my eyes.

Caleb is walking away. His shoulders are hunched up to his

ears and his head is down, and his hands are curled up into tight fists at his sides.

My whole world cracks at the seams, like a gulf the size of the Grand Canyon just opened between us.

I'm frozen in place, watching his retreating back as I desperately try to think what I should do.

If I run after him, is he going to tell me those words I dread hearing all over again?

We're done. It's over. You're out.

Does he want me to chase him? Should I give him time to think about it? How much time do we have before the show? Does he even want to do it anymore?

Too many questions bombard me at once. I press my hand against the glass window to keep myself upright as my whole body sags like I got hit in the stomach.

"Caleb," I croak. But he doesn't turn around.

Oh, fuck. What have I done?

Everything was going too well. I should have known. God damn it, I should have *known*.

For a brief, glorious day, I thought my life was going the way I'd always dreamed.

My family is going to be out there in the audience tonight, finally supporting me in my dreams instead of making snarky comments about my poetry. Even Gary agreed to come tonight, and he said he was looking forward to it.

And I had a boyfriend who seemed to give a shit. So much for that. Was he organizing this whole thing as some kind of career comeback, fresh start thing for himself?

I should have seen it coming a mile off. My life isn't a fucking fairytale, and nobody wants to help you out for nothing. Even if they're getting trophy videos out of it.

I feel disgusted—and disgusting.

The tears don't stay inside for long. I don't even make it to the staircase up to my apartment before I'm a snotty mess, my eyes so blurred that I trip twice. I choke on the adrenaline as the bitter sting surges into my mouth again.

I don't know how I manage to get my key into the lock, much

less the door open. I slam it after me and collapse onto the floor, unable to make it even one step more.

Then the grief of betrayal overflows my chest into every finger and toe of my body. I pull my knees to my chest and press my face into them as the choked, wretched sobbing starts.

I'm mortified. How didn't I recognize him? Thank God I wasn't a Jet Slack fan, but of course I've seen his face in music videos online and in the newspaper when the band fractured.

That was *him*? The troubled rock star who got kicked out of his own band a few years ago? I don't remember much about it, but everyone heard. It was one of those things that was hot news for all of thirty seconds.

Why the hell didn't he tell me?

I can't swallow back the shame. I'm a total amateur, some guy with a couple of okay poems, and he's this global superstar. God, I'm mortified. He must have been laughing at me all along, getting stage fright about being in front of twenty people.

This is some fun little game to him. Deflowering a shy little virgin, making him think he's some big star, all the while neglecting to mention that he's this big shot.

But it's my life and I wanted to take my own tiny little life, my own modest dreams, seriously. How can I when compared to a guy whose voice I've heard on the radio for years?

God, now that I know, I even recognize the warm hum of his words. It's different than in their songs, but it seems so stupidly obvious.

I want to crawl into a hole and die of embarrassment. But I can't. I can't just sit around here on my floor feeling sorry for myself.

Or can I? It's really fucking tempting, I won't lie.

My phone vibrates, and as much as I want to ignore it, I can't help slipping it out of my pocket.

It's Tag.

I'm sorry. I'll be at V&V all night.

He's not pressuring me into coming back to do my thing. But neither is he coming after me. Crap. I don't know *what* I want, but I know I feel like he just stabbed a knife in my back right before my big break.

Does he have an ulterior motive? Does he just want the show to go on like normal? He's good with an audience—surely he could spin it into his own thing if he didn't care.

I don't know. I'm all mixed up, and I have no idea what he's thinking. I can only focus on how bad this hurts.

But this is the opportunity I've been waiting for. No matter how much Tag lied to me about who he is, this is supposed to be my night. My whole family is there and this is finally my chance to prove that I'm serious about it.

If I blow off tonight, everyone will think I don't have the guts for it. That I'm not a real performer. And I might not be some award-winning rock star, but I believe in myself.

Or… I was starting to learn to, anyway.

My phone goes off again, and when I look at the screen, it's Lee.

Lee: *Good luck tonight! I see Tag, but he says you're not here yet?*

Fuck. And of all my brothers, it had to be Lee. I press the edge of my phone to my forehead and groggily pull myself to my feet, leaning against the doorway.

Even seeing the man's name makes me choke. I avert my gaze as I tap a response on the keyboard.

Me: *I don't know if I can.*

Then my phone buzzes again.

Lee: *You can do it, little bro. You've always done your own thing no matter what anyone says.*

I stare at the screen, unable to come up with a response. An explanation. A cry for help. I don't know what.

Another message.

Lee: *I tease you a lot, but I like Tag and he's been good for you. I'm really proud of you. Come on down and give us what you've got.*

Another strangled sob emerges. I want to tell him—but I don't want to out Tag, even with how badly he's hurt me. I'm not going to be that kind of person.

Besides, Tag said he was afraid of me outing him to the whole town. That means I can't turn around and do it, proving him right. I have to prove that I'm a better person than he thought. I can keep his secret *and* be really, really pissed off at him at the same time.

It takes every ounce of my strength, but I tap out two letters.

Me: *OK.*

Then I pocket my phone and press the heels of my hands into my eyes. I can do this. I have to do this.

I'm going to pull myself together and make myself and my family proud, even if I have to grit my teeth the whole time to do it.

I stride to the coffee table where all the poems I decided not to read are still spread out, and drop heavily onto the couch. Then I grab a pen and a blank piece of paper.

Maybe I'm not really interesting or pretty enough to be heard after all. Tag made me think otherwise for a few brief, perfect days. But I'm still going to be me—without apology and without limits.

Nobody is going to hold me down or keep me back anymore. Didn't I promise myself that just minutes ago? It feels like another lifetime, like a sharp divide has fallen between that part of my life and this one.

But I always keep my promises. Always.

24

TAG

I should have listened to my gut.

From the very start, I didn't feel right about not telling Caleb who I used to be. I justified it, but deep down I knew he'd be hurt when he finally found out.

Now all I can do is pace along the wall of Vino and Veritas, looking foreboding enough that nobody has tried to approach me apart from Lee. Even he quickly beat a retreat after asking where Caleb is.

I don't even remember what I said five seconds ago. Hopefully I gave him an answer instead of just grunting at him, *Fuck if I know.*

I hope Caleb will come back. I could talk quietly to Tanner and apologize for screwing up the plan, but there's no way I can make up some bullshit that Caleb's friends and family would believe.

Okay. If I need to, I'll be honest: that I did something dumb and I'm not sure if Caleb is coming tonight, but please enjoy this complimentary mead or something. I don't know. I'll find a way to make up for it to the audience tonight.

Nobody here is as important as the one man who *isn't* here.

I guess I could just leave, but… no. I've already been enough of a coward. There's no way in hell I'd ever do that.

I'm going to keep my word and stay all night—until closing time, if I have to—just to give Caleb the chance to come back to me on his own terms. Assuming he ever wants to see me again.

I think I can safely guess whether we're boyfriends anymore based on whether or not he shows up. It might be the longest night of my life.

I pace another circuit of the walls, steering neatly around anyone who tries to stop me. I can't stop glancing at my watch, counting down the minutes. I can always give it an extra five minutes before hopping on stage and saying…

Well, I've got seven minutes to figure out what to say. No, six minutes now.

The door opens.

I've long since stopped spinning around to look at the door every time someone walks through. It was going to give me a heart attack if I kept that up.

But this time is different. It's seven o'clock on the dot, and all the hair stands up on the back of my neck. A second later, I hear greetings and a smattering of applause. Even a little cheer. That's Anna, who's sitting in the front row with a big glass of mead.

So I finally give in and spin around, my stomach turning itself inside out.

It's him. It's Caleb. His face is a little blotchy and his eyes are too pink, but he's holding himself upright with his chest out and his chin up. More like he's ready for battle than a casual poetry reading.

"Let's go," is all he says to me as he walks past to the stage.

My heart drops like a stone into my shoes.

We're done, he might as well have told me. There's no way he would have walked right past me if…

Shut up, I tell my brain. *Switch off and do this.*

And this isn't the first time.

I was the one who decided to throw the setlist out the window in that very last concert. It was a small, intimate gig in a little bar in Denver. Just for our superfans, the ones who waited up all night to grab tickets from the secret email list.

There was never going to be a better moment, so I pulled the most diva of diva moves for a lead singer. The rest of the band were forced to accompany me like it was all planned in advance.

I told the crowd that they were going to hear something new, and I launched into the song that I wrote—that I was *sure* would push us in a new direction. None of my bandmates agreed. They wanted to keep singing the same shit, acting like the same idiots, while I wanted to be *real* with the people who most understood us.

Well, it was two and a half minutes of joy. The fans loved it, I loved it, and all my bandmates kept up with the verses I'd forced them to learn, however much they told me they wouldn't be caught dead doing it.

For those two and a half minutes, I dared to dream that we were going to strike out in the right direction at last.

Then my backup singer took the mic, and the consequences bit me in the ass. Hard.

We've got some news to share, and we wanted you to be the first to know. There's no good way to say this, but… that was a farewell song just for you guys. Tonight was Titus' last performance with Jet Slack. After so many great years with us, he's heading in a new direction. I know. We're all upset, too. One more? You all want one more? Okay. Let's do the last song, guys.

He didn't even look me in the fucking eye. Not once. Stone cold sober ripped my heart out on stage and stomped on it.

I don't even remember if I sang the right words in that finale. Everyone was crying and shouting that they loved me and shit. It was no real consolation. Nothing could possibly soothe the biggest shock of my life.

I've never fought so hard to keep a mask on. Not until tonight.

I'd forgotten what that felt like and now I wish I couldn't remember anything at all, ever again. The old wounds are bleeding, and my stomach hurts so bad that I want to throw up.

How many times can I screw up? Will I just keep running away from a good thing, sabotaging myself over and over, for my whole life?

Once more, I have to flash a winning smile and strut onto stage like nothing's wrong.

He doesn't stop for an intermission, either. Caleb just nails poem after poem. There's an intensity to his face and words, a total focus. Like a motherfucking professional, he times and pitches every word perfectly.

The audience is in the palm of his hand, and so am I… but the bittersweet irony hurts so badly. There he is—the performer and the man I always knew he could be. He's found himself at the exact moment I've lost him.

Then he comes to the last poem, and I catch a glimpse sideways at the handwritten scrawl.

That's new. All the other poems are printed out.

Oh, no. I know what this is before he can say a single word. It's the slap I deserve, delivered in the style only Caleb could manage.

The last snowflake doesn't come
with a label, no warning bell.
Just a still gray sky closing
the door and turning away.
Beneath, a sea of its wealth
spread out, spent flakes pressed
under each other's weight
as they sink, gasping, into earth.

Every snow angel melts one day,
yet each winter we make them
again, as if outrunning fate.
But one flake will always be the last,
drifting to the ground alone,
for brief moments that are

its forever, whispering

a fragile goodbye.

There's no way I could miss his meaning.

It's over. Tonight, and… and us.

Oh, fuck.

Ice and heat flood me at once, and my eyes burn. My throat is tight. Thank God I don't have to say another word. When Caleb steps off the stage and the applause starts, I smile and try to pretend that I can feel my palms making contact with each other.

But all I can feel is the chill of the winter night outside settling into my bones, and a thousand more to come without Caleb by my side.

If this pain is like melting snow, shouldn't I grow mercifully numb? Yet still, I'm forced to *feel*.

I slowly walk down the stairs, trying not to look at Caleb joining his family. They're smiling and clapping his shoulders, voices raised and enthusiastic.

Everyone is in awe, showering him with the love he deserves. And if I hadn't fucked up so badly I could be right there along with him, telling him how proud I am of him.

Instead, as Lee gestures for me to join in, I pick my way through the crowd. Caleb will know where I am.

I make a beeline to the table at the back of the room where we had our first date. I lean on it casually, because I'm not sure I could get up again if he doesn't join me.

I'm pretty sure I saw Rod in the audience, but he must know better than to approach me. I've never been a man for violence, but I might well consider it.

No. My shoulders sink. I can't even take comfort in that tiny daydream. I know damn well it's not his fault. It was bound to happen. If not him, someone would have seen me someday.

This is squarely my fault.

Movement catches my eye by the door, and I can't help looking. Accompanied by Lee, followed by all the rest of his brothers and sisters-in-law and parents… Caleb walks out the front door of the bar. He doesn't look back.

And that's the moment my heart breaks—for good.

25

CALEB

When everything else in my life is shit, my spreadsheets are predictable and comfortable.

All week in the office, I've been volunteering for extra work. Throwing myself headlong into the most boring reports—even the ones macros would probably handle just fine. Anything that will narrow down the world to just me, a computer screen, and a column of stable, solid, *easy* numbers.

I can't believe it's Friday now. I'm weirdly disappointed. Without work to distract me, two painful weekend days stretch ahead of me, and they're totally empty of plans.

I've already excused myself from family dinner this week, because I can't stand one more pitying look. Even Gary keeps looking at me like he's not sure if he should be taking the staplers and pushpins out of my desk.

If he does, hopefully he'll do me a favor and empty out *that* drawer at the same time.

On Tuesday morning, I shoved all my lunchtime scrawling into the bottom drawer in my desk. Four days later, I still haven't even managed to open it. I tell myself it's because I'm going to wait for the right moment to have some, like, ritual burning ceremony.

"Coming for lunch?" Gary usually lets my coworkers do their own thing at lunch. But it's one of those rare days when everyone's going out together.

"No, thanks." I keep on typing, but I don't hear footsteps receding yet.

I swallow a sigh and roll back to look around the edge of the cubicle. He's giving me that concerned look again. "Are you sure?"

"I'm meeting with my brother for lunch," I promise him. "I'm good."

The relief on his face is plain. "Oh. Okay, good. Don't hurry back if you don't want to. There's nothing urgent right now."

Gary means well, so I resist the urge to complain. But more time off is the opposite of what I want. I hope he finds some last-minute project that only I can do. Even better if it takes up my whole weekend.

"Thanks," I tell Gary and wave goodbye, rolling back to my desk.

I can finish this column before I shut down my computer and join Kelvin at the maple café. He'll probably show up late anyway. He always lets appointments run over time. It's one of many reasons his patients and their parents love him.

After saving everything, I shut down my computer. When I turn to grab my jacket, I flinch at the sight. It's still too fresh—yet all the memories from just last weekend feel like they happened to a different man.

One who was too damn naive and trusting for his own good.

I shrug on the blue puffy jacket and zip it up so aggressively I almost get my throat caught. "I'm not buying a new one," I tell myself with a scowl. Just because it reminds me of making snow angels, laughing until I cry, and having the time of my life... that's not a good reason to spend good money on a new jacket.

Besides, he shouldn't be able to invade every little bit of my life. But that won't stop him.

Tag's like the fuse in an electric circuit. He lives in the little spaces of my body and mind that I never knew were empty until we met. No matter how hard I've been trying, I can't just cut him out of my thoughts and pretend it never happened.

It doesn't work that way. Not for me, anyway.

As soon as I push open the door of the café, I see Kelvin at a table with two maple crullers and two cups of green tea.

Oh, God. For a moment, it hurts so bad I can't breathe.

But then he looks over and smiles and waves, so I force myself to raise a hand and wave back like my heart isn't shattering.

Damn stupid, fragile thing. I've duct-taped it together with blood, sweat and tears this week. And still, the slightest reminder is enough to devastate me all over again.

"Hey," Kelvin greets me by rising to his feet for a half-hug. It lasts a little longer than usual, and it's impossible to miss the eye he casts over me.

"I'm okay, before you ask," I tell him with a brief squeeze around his shoulders. Then I pull away and sit down. "And I don't want to talk about him."

"Okay." Kelvin sits down, picks up his donut, and settles back in his own chair to eat it a bite at a time.

It takes about ten seconds.

"I just wish I knew why he did it." I stare into my cup of tea as I wrap my fingers around it like I'm trying to soak up all the heat. "But if I meet him... oh, God. I don't know if I can stay mad at him."

Kelvin knows better than to ask what I mean. I haven't told them a word about what Tag's secret was. Only that he wasn't the guy I thought he was.

"Do you *want* to stay mad?" Kelvin's got his professional voice on, but I'm too tired of my own brain to be annoyed.

"Yes." Then I grimace. "No, not exactly. I'm just holding onto the anger because... what else have I got?"

"A new career?" Kelvin shrugs.

I snort. "Yeah, right. I haven't written anything since... the snowflake poem."

His lips twitch. "I'll hand it to you, that one took balls. But why would you let him stop you from doing something you love?"

Irritation sparks in my chest. "I'm not *letting* him stop me from anything. I just… I'm afraid that if I let go of all that anger, I'll find out that I still want him."

Crap. My mouth got ahead of my brain, and now that the words are out there I can't take them back. I have to process them at the same time that Kelvin does. Am I really that hung up on him?

Yeah. I am.

"What's so bad about that?" Kelvin slowly asks. He holds up a hand. "I mean, to me, he's a genuine guy. If he'd just wanted to get it over with, he could have come to dinner and sat there like a rock for a few hours."

I swallow the lump in my tight throat. Yeah, he seemed to be trying hard, which makes this suck even more. "Then why not just… be upfront from the beginning?"

Then I wince. I haven't told my brothers his secret identity. All I said was that they were right and Tag wasn't being honest about who he was.

"He… used to be someone else. He moved here to escape his past. But why didn't he tell me when things got serious?"

Kelvin looks at me like he's not sure I'll like the answer. So I sigh and wave for him to say it anyway, shoving the maple donut in my mouth.

"I'm not making fun of you, I promise. But Caleb, it was only a week, wasn't it?"

I glower. It's a good thing for him that my mouth is full of donut, and I'm not risking a test of his Heimlich maneuver.

My heart was on the line from day one. We both knew that. The intensity of our relationship had nothing to do with the time and everything to do with how fast we both opened up.

Or I *thought* we both opened up.

Kelvin chuckles like he can read my face. "No, I'm not saying it should hurt less. But listen. Say he's got this past he doesn't want people here knowing about. I don't know what, and I'm not asking. But maybe he just didn't expect to fall for you so fast."

I grimace. "He did claim that he was about to tell me. But don't people always say that when they get caught in a lie?"

"Little brother, you don't have nearly enough worldly experience to be that cynical," Kelvin informs me. "Stop taking other people's fears on board—even mine. Tag seemed to be trying to show you that much, and I approved." Then he points a finger at me while I gape at him like a mortally offended fish. "You're lucky. You've always known who you are. You could have tried to imitate one of us growing up, and you didn't. You know how rare that is in little siblings?"

"Yes, Dr. Expert Face," I grumble, trying to hide my smile.

Kelvin laughs and kicks me under the table. "I'm serious. I'm not saying you should chase him down and get engaged next week. Some time and space is probably what you need. But maybe… just maybe… he cares *so much* that he was afraid of what you'd think."

"What *I* think?" I squeak before clearing my throat. Kelvin has no idea who Tag really is. He's sold out stadiums and won awards and… why the hell would he care what little old me thinks?

The answer comes to me before I even finish the question. *Because he doesn't see me as little old me.*

Damn it. Kelvin is right.

"I should have talked to Eli. *He'd* have helped me kick the guy in the balls," I sigh.

Kelvin winks. "Yeah. That's why I'm getting in there first. Mom and Dad want grandkids from all of us."

My jaw drops as I stare at him again, the cup of green tea halfway between the table and my mouth. "*Kev.*"

He just drains his cup and stands up. "It's true. Anyway, I hate to run, but I'm squeezing a couple extra lunchtime appointments in. Think about it, won't you? At the very least, you're going to keep writing poetry if we have to chain you to a notepad."

"I…" I rub my temple and slowly shake my head. "Yeah. I will," I mumble. "Thanks?"

I've never come to lunch to be attacked so thoroughly, but I'm secretly glad that Kelvin is happy to say what I need to hear. Not to try to get a rise from me like Lee and Eli, but because it's best for me.

"You're welcome." He squeezes my shoulder and then strides off with another goodbye wave.

Then I'm alone with half a cruller and a cup of barely-touched tea, and a whole new set of problems.

But my office is empty and quiet right now. By the time I get there I'll still have thirty minutes or more before my coworkers interrupt—probably longer, since Gary's with them. There's a poem fermenting in my fingertips, and it's just about ready to come out.

I shove the rest of my donut in my mouth and snap the lid on my paper cup, then hurry for the door.

Kelvin's right. I can't stop loving what I love just because I got hurt.

26

TAG

Sitting on an upturned bucket inside the disconnected electric fence, I watch the comings and goings of the bees in my home apiary: six hives clustered close together.

What else do I have to do? The feeding stage is over for my new batch of mead. I have enough bottled cases in my makeshift warehouse to meet orders. I could try to develop new recipes, but I'm not feeling it right now.

But it's the kind of day when autumn hasn't quite given up against winter's ravages. A few inches of snow are underfoot, but clear blue sky and warm sunshine makes it feel warm enough that I've unzipped my thick plaid hoodie.

I'm sitting to one side of the hive entrances so I don't irritate them, and from this angle I can clearly see the fuzzy little bees emerge, swoop up in the air for a quick circle around, and return.

This isn't just a casual stretch of the wings they're doing. The polite term is "elimination flights," and the snow in front of the hives is covered in tiny dots of bee poop. Suffice it to say that I can't eat black-flecked vanilla bean ice cream without closing my eyes.

As a beekeeper, I'd prefer it if winter set in quickly and stayed a steady temperature below freezing until spring. That way they'll go into hibernation and eat less, and I won't worry so much about feeding them. But it's nice to hear them humming with life.

Makes me feel a little less alone.

As each bee circles around, she tries to make her way back to her own hive. Normally they're pretty good at finding home, and we paint hives different colors to help. But they're all wrapped in black plastic to help keep them warm, so the bees can get lost sometimes.

As soon as they land at a hive entrance, bees will rush forward and put their legs and antennae all over them, sniffing their returning sisters to make sure they belong here. If they smell wrong, they're kicked out—literally.

In beekeeping courses, I learned that sometimes the guards will let a lost bee past the defenses, as long as they aren't here to raid their honey stores. Gradually the chemical scent on the newcomer will change as the new hive adopts them, and then it's like they've always belonged there.

Wouldn't it be nice if humans worked that way? But I feel like however long I'm here in Vermont, I'll always be on the outside looking in. They might pretend to let me in, but I'm not one of *them*.

It's going to be dark before long. The days are already growing shorter, and as the warm afternoon cools off, the hive activity will drop too.

I sigh and push myself to my feet, stretching out my stiff knees. My ass is numb from the little plastic circle I've been sitting on. I leave the bucket where it is and reconnect the wires of the electric fence, then switch it on. Once it's softly clicking again, I trudge up through the snowy field to the house.

Last I saw, Queenie was asleep on her back in front of the fireplace, paws dangling over her chest and tongue lolling.

She's got the right idea. That's basically what I've been doing for the last week, barely leaving the house.

Just a couple of deliveries to restaurants and bars, and one grocery trip. Nobody's said a peep about the big revelation and I haven't seen any of those shy-yet-excited looks that mean I've been spotted.

Obviously if anyone overheard that asshole blurting it out for the whole world, they're keeping it to themselves. I feel bad for underestimating the locals… especially Caleb.

I can't stop thinking about him. Every night when I go to bed alone, I close the blinds. I can't stand to open my eyes in the middle of the night only to see the moonbeam illuminating an empty bed.

It hurts all the more because I know I'm the one who screwed up, bad. I could have been honest, and I was too scared.

No wonder Caleb wants nothing to do with me.

Another call comes in, but I don't bother answering my vibrating pocket. I let it go to voicemail. I know exactly who it is, and it's not Caleb calling to give me a second chance.

I changed his ringtone, just in case.

It'll be Rod—again. He calls at least twice a day and leaves voicemails. He left town a few days ago, but not before tracking down my phone number. God only knows how.

"Hungry young agent" is one way of describing him. "Tick burrowing under my skin" is a better way.

I've listened to his messages while rolling my eyes so hard I might sprain them. He keeps asking to meet up or video conference, offering me the world. He claims to have so many opportunities for exposure. Well, out here in the Vermont woods, you die of exposure.

Only after I've shrugged off my hoodie and gotten comfortable on the couch do I pull out my phone. I play the voicemail, just for kicks.

"Hey. It's Rod. So I was thinking, you seem pretty comfy in your life here. But man, you don't have to give that up. I wanna help you out. We can re-embrace your real talent while you keep doing your quirky… 'thing' out here."

I snort. He thinks I'm a total wacko, but a cash cow for him.

"Give me a call. I know you've still got it in you, Titus. Or Tag. Whatever. Call me. Bye."

I press the delete key before the voicemail can even prompt me, then hang up and toss my hone on the couch next to me.

"What an ass."

Queenie grumbles as she stirs, flailing all her limbs in different directions and staring dramatically at me.

I laugh and pick up my phone to snap a photo for Caleb before I remember. Then my shoulders sag and I drop it next to me again, running my hands along my face.

I need to let it go—let Caleb go. He's made his lack of interest very clear. But I can't. I just can't stop thinking about him. I'm freaking stuck on him and I'm terrified I might *stay* stuck.

I love him, plain and simple. That's the worst part of all of this. When he walked away, he took my heart with him.

The feelings between us might have developed quickly, but that doesn't mean they'll fade anytime soon. It's going to be a long damn time before I can get out of bed without hurting all over.

That ache settles into my bones, weighing me down on the couch for... I don't even know how much time passes. Queenie naps, I stare into space and occasionally throw another log on the fire, and darkness falls.

It's not until my stomach grumbles that I remember it's Sunday: open mic night.

Ouch.

If it were *just* numbness and desolation, I could maybe deal with it. Or if it were *just* the sharp stabbing pain of despair, I could figure that out. But this ever-changing cloud of grief constantly finds the most effective way to haunt me.

It was only two weeks ago that we met. But I can't bring myself to wish I hadn't even gone that night. I'm glad he gave me the chance to love him. I'm just angry I didn't do the right thing, and now I can't go back and erase my mistakes.

The night we met, I was probably right not to leap into telling

Caleb everything. But I had so many chances that I ignored or stifled because—under all my excuses—I was just flat-out afraid.

I presented Caleb a perfect image of a loner beekeeper with a simple life, and I thought that was who he loved. I didn't want to do anything to screw it up. He was totally honest from the very first moment, while I created a persona all over again. A fake, just like the onstage persona that I've tried so hard to leave in the past.

I have to go.

I don't know why I do it. I shouldn't want to be there again. But I can't just sit around staring at the walls for weeks on end, hoping that this pain will get better. I already know it won't.

All I can do is *try*, and hope.

So I drive to Vino and Veritas, and I park in the same place as before, and I slip through the front door and walk straight to that table at the back.

And when I look toward the stage, all of a sudden a chill runs down my spine. It's the same kind of feeling I had that very first night: like fate is whispering in my ear.

It's Caleb, and his golden curls and deep eyes and every freckle I didn't get a chance to kiss.

I got here just in time to see him walk toward the microphone holding a sheet of paper.

I can't breathe. I can't even think straight. My whole world narrows to Caleb and Caleb alone. I have no idea who's working behind the bar tonight, or who else is in the crowd. Like tunnel vision, all I can see is the stage, and the man on it.

I thought my heart was too broken to feel it anymore, but here it is again, thumping in my ears so loudly I can hardly hear his voice as he says something.

I'd do anything—*anything*—to get another chance. Come on, universe. Come on, Caleb. Whoever I need to beg or pray to, I'll do it.

This time I'll get it right.

CALEB

"Just the one poem today," I tell the crowd with a little smile. I flick my gaze around a few random people near the front, and I'm amazed at how… *easy* this feels.

There's no paralysis anymore. I'm not terrified that I'll screw up. Because it's not like I've got anything to gain or lose. I've already won the world and walked away from it. From *him*.

I draw a breath and start to read.

What dreams has a winter bee,
gorged on honey, trembling softly
with her sisters through the night?

Does she remember nectar,
the sun above, still lakes,
soft wind amidst the storm?

The last blossom shakes off
the snow and seeks its angel,
a glass slipper in the cold.

Forced apart by the seasons,

they wait through fading light
for a chance to meet anew.

I look up from the page to a handful of perplexed faces. People don't seem quite sure whether to applaud. And I can't say I blame them. Despite a weekend rewriting this poem, it's still pretty bad.

But that's okay. It wasn't written for anyone who's here tonight. It's more important that I get back on the horse and learn to bare my heart again.

I smile and fold up the paper, shoving it into my pocket. "Thank you," I lean in and say to the microphone.

And then my eyes land on him, just as the polite applause starts.

I was wrong. My angel *is* here. He's sitting at that table all the way in the back. My eyes meet his, and a jolt shivers through my whole body.

Tag.

I can't tear my eyes away. This time, he doesn't move a muscle as I walk off the stage. He just sits there, watching me like he's afraid to hope.

So am I.

I make a beeline through the crowd, heading straight for him.

Ever since my conversation with Kelvin, I've been thinking about Tag—about *us*. Hours spent hunched over the page, crossing out stanzas and muttering aloud, yet he's never far from my mind.

Maybe he lied, but maybe I wasn't fair to him either. Tag believed in me from the moment we met, and he's always tried to help me succeed. I don't think he was trying to revive his career. Why would he do it at a poetry night in a little bar under a different name?

The more I thought about it, the more I realized that he was always holding a little piece of himself back. I sensed it, but I was so eager to believe that he was my fairytale ending. Maybe he still is—but not because of his fame or money. He's a knight with battle-worn armor, and I just want his love.

"Tag," I whisper as I stumble to a halt in front of the table.

He's risen to his feet, staring at me like he can't believe I'm real. "Caleb," he breathes hoarsely.

A few seconds pass. It hurts, the gulf between us. I want to reach out and smooth his lapels, or cup his cheeks and kiss him, or... anything.

I sink into one chair, and Tag gulps and sits opposite me again. "Are you the bee or the flower in that poem?"

I shake my head. "I don't know. Maybe I'm Cinderella and I want my shoe back. My *heart* back." My voice feels raw.

"Do you really?" Tag asks softly. "Or do you just want me to take more care with it?"

I make a face. He knows the answer as well as I do. "That last one."

Tag swallows and nods hard, and I scrutinize him. He looks tired. Obviously he hasn't been sleeping well. But he also can't stop watching me with a painfully honest mix of eagerness and trepidation.

I recognize the famous guy now in the shape of his face, but he doesn't look like the guy I looked up on Google. Not anymore. I see Tag, not that Titus guy on the album covers and in the promo photos.

I don't give a crap about the fame or the money or any of it. I just want that guy *I* know back—the one who cooks me breakfast in bed and looks at me like I'm the most precious thing alive.

The way he's looking at me now.

God, he must be so jaded and tired of people who see all that other stuff first. Like that agent, or whoever he really was, Rod. I hated him from first sight. If that's the way people usually react to Tag, no wonder he was afraid about telling me.

I just wish he'd given me a chance first.

"I miss you," I murmur at last as the breath rushes out of me. "Everything I write is shit. Did you hear that?" I gesture at the stage as a pained little smile curves my lips. "I'm not gonna make a career out of that."

Tag doesn't say anything. He just watches me, his eyes those same deep, earnest pools that I learned to trust.

"I can't think straight, and I can't sleep, and…" I rest my elbows on the table and run my hands through my hair.

Then I look up at him again, watching him bite his lip so hard it turns white.

"I want to know the truth," I whisper with a little shake of my head. "All of it, however ugly. I'll be brave if you are. Can you promise me that?"

My heart is pounding a dance floor rhythm against my ribcage. Everything depends on Tag's next words.

Tag reaches across the table with both hands, laying them flat and palm-up between us. His eyes are an open invitation—a plea. My head is a mess, but my heart knows what to do.

I let out my breath and straighten up, placing my trembling hands into his palms.

The moment I do, both of us let out a breath as the muscles in our bodies loosen. Sparks still tremble through my hands at his touch, and *rightness* settles into my body once more.

Tag closes his warm fingers around my hands and nods, squeezing tight. "It's a deal," he says. My eyes mist up when his voice cracks on the last word.

I swallow hard and raise Tag's hands, pressing my lips to them one at a time. "Deal. Now, take me home." I mean his home, of course—the place I could grow to think of as *our* home.

And judging by the smile on Tag's face as he rises to his feet, he knows exactly what I mean.

28

TAG

Over a glass of mead in my tasting room, I tell Caleb everything.

And I mean everything. From the first wild idea that we should start a band to the parties, the awards snubs and the antagonistic interviewers, I don't hold back.

Even when it comes to the end. *Especially* the end.

"He just threw you out… live, on stage… without even talking to the others?" Caleb's cheeks are pale with horror as he stares at me, transfixed.

I bite my lip. "No. That's the worst part. They were all on the same page. So they must have already been talking about it."

"*Ohhh.*" Caleb breathes a long, low groan. It's a little bit distracting, in a pleasant way—and I can use all the distraction I can get.

"They were just waiting for me to break a contract term so they could screw me over. I should never have gone rogue and given them the chance."

"Or…" Caleb murmurs, his brows furrowing. "Maybe they were planning to do it that night anyway. That's why they were all ready for it. I don't know."

My mouth opens and then closes silently as my head spins. It takes me a good few seconds to even wrap my brain around what he's saying.

How is it that a legal battle, emotional breakdown, and four years have gone by and I've never once thought of that possibility?

The answer is obvious: because I've been blaming myself all along. Telling myself it was *my* fault for being too authentic, that nobody wants the *real* me. That I get to be either loved or authentic, but never both.

I never even stopped to consider the fact that they might have been planning this all along. Why else would they have agreed to my suggestion of a small, intimate superfans-only concert? And learned the music I nagged them to learn, despite warning me we'd never play it?

Holy shit.

I close my eyes. I want to call Roxy and find out if she knew. No, there's no need. She couldn't have hid it from me. And she isn't our boss. She works for us—*for them*, I remind myself—so they wouldn't have needed to involve her.

Besides, she was in shock, too. I still remember Roxy's expression because she was the first person I saw when we stepped off stage. And she was the only one who looked like I felt. The rest of those dickheads and the lawyers seemed like they were ready for me… because they were, one way or another.

Caleb's right. They were going to fire me anyway.

Suddenly, a weight lifts off my shoulders—one I didn't know I've been carrying around for years. It would have ended that night no matter what, and I went out on my terms, not theirs.

"Are you okay?" Caleb murmurs. He slides closer to me on the padded bench, slipping his arm around my shoulders.

"I will be." I turn my face to his and close my eyes, letting him press his lips to mine. It's sweet and tender, a slow exploration of this new relationship we're rebuilding.

This time, we're doing the right thing from the start. *I'm* doing the right thing, that is. Caleb sees all of me, all the things I did and the person I pretended to be, and he hasn't even flinched.

He still wants me, and I'll never take that for granted.

The kiss lingers for precious seconds, deepening slowly into a raw-edged promise of all the things we have yet to share—and then my phone goes off.

Caleb jumps and breaks away from me with a sharp little gasp, then giggles. "Sorry. Startled me."

"God. That asshole again, I bet." I scowl as I shove my hand in my pocket to fish out my phone.

Rod isn't going to go away on his own. As long as he thinks I'm just waiting for the right offer, he's going to keep bugging me. I have to make it clear that that life is over for me.

And now I know for sure that it is.

Maybe that's why I didn't outright turn Rod down until now. A part of me was still afraid, keeping a single toe in the door... just in case. If I was about to lose everything here, I had an escape route.

But I don't need one. Caleb accepts me for who I am.

"Rod," I answer, bringing the phone to my ear.

"Oh! You're there!" Rod sounds shocked to actually hear me.

"Lose my number," I tell him. "I'm not interested. I have a life here, and I'm not leaving it behind for the world. And I don't care if you say I can do two things at once—that's not the way I am. I'm all-in here."

There's silence from the other end. I'm not even sure he's still there until he splutters a little cough. "But think of the money you could make—"

I laugh. Even if I *were* still interested, that's the worst angle he could have taken. He should have done his homework first. Roxy would have told him that for free.

"All the money *you* can make?" I counter. "No, thanks. I'm done. If I ever change my mind, I'm going to find someone who respects my right to privacy."

Rod's voice turns ugly. "Fine. You don't need to be such a dick about it."

"Apparently I do. Bye, Rod. Good luck."

I hang up and slap my phone on the table, looking at Caleb.

"Better?" He grins at me.

I beam back at him. "Oh, yeah. I should have done that days ago." That felt incredible.

"You weren't ready then." His hand slips into mine and he squeezes gently. "Things happen when they're meant to."

"Mmm. So wise. What do I pay for the life advice?" I stroke the back of his hand with a fingertip.

"A Poet."

"That's *who* I pay—oh! The cocktail." I grin and throw myself to my feet, striding toward the bar.

Whatever Caleb asks for, he'll get.

I fetch eggs from the fridge in my kitchen before hurrying back out to the tasting room. A tiny part of me is scared that when I open the door again, he'll be gone.

Like a mirage that's too good to be true melting into the earth.

But no… there he is, patiently waiting exactly where I left him thirty seconds ago, hands folded in his lap and a little smile on his lips. "Hi."

I let out a breath and close the door with my shoulder. "Hey. Two Poets coming right up."

"Speaking of which, I never got to hear your poetry," Caleb prompts me with a grin.

I chuckle. "It's just as well. It really is awful. I'm going to burn it in the fireplace." He gasps, but I shake my head. "Trust me. I'm done with all of it. I was only holding onto it because I was still…" I shrug, cracking the eggs one at a time. "Bitter, I guess."

Caleb props his chin on his fist. "Mmm. And you aren't now?"

"Why would I be?" I smile at him. "Everything that's happened has led me here. As far as I'm concerned, it's pretty damn sweet."

I'm done being in the limelight. Instead, I'm going to support Caleb to stand in it for as long as he wants.

If a tear slips down my cheek as I channel all that excitement for the future into shaking and pouring our cocktails, Caleb pretends not to notice. Once I sit down and slide him his cocktail, he holds up his glass and I gently clink mine against it. "A toast? You pick."

I swallow hard. "To the music we'll write together."

Then we both sip, and he moans softly. "Delicious. Thank you. So, are you going to write more songs?"

I shake my head. "I don't think so. I'm happier singing other people's words."

He giggles softly. "Like my poems? Nah, that would be weird."

But I'm grinning and standing up, already taking the guitar down from the wall. I have to scoot the table back carefully and turn at an angle so I can rest it in my lap.

"Give me your poem again. One line at a time. The mountains one."

Caleb smiles so hard his little dimples appear. "From the first night?"

"Mmhmm."

One line at a time, he murmurs the words and then waits. I close my eyes and let the chords flow through my fingers, picking out the notes of a soft and dreamy tune.

And I repeat after him, but instead of speaking, I sing his words and let them drift through the air in the peaks and valleys they deserve. Not all the lines work perfectly, but when it sounds particularly strange, we both just laugh together.

By the last line, I'm gazing into his eyes, strumming that very last chord.

How far could I bear to fall?

Caleb leans in over my guitar, and I let it sit in my lap as I reach out for his cheeks instead, cupping them between my warm palms.

"I love you," I whisper.

He makes a choking little sound as he flings his arms around my shoulders. "I love you, too," he murmurs against my lips, and then kisses me with a soft desperation I can't help but meet.

The kiss goes on and on, and it takes everything I have to even let us pause for breath. I just want to press myself against him until we've lost ourselves—every trace of our past gone, swallowed by each other's love and the future we're going to find together.

Both of us are teary by the time we pull apart. I clear my throat and pinch the bridge of my nose.

"You have to play at open mic night sometime," Caleb whispers, his voice rough. He clears his throat and wipes his eyes. "Unless… you think people would recognize you?"

I snort. "Screw it. I'm done hiding. All that matters is that you don't mind."

Caleb shakes his head and smiles. "You're just Tag," he murmurs and kisses me again. "I want a happy Tag."

I laugh and brush two fingers fondly under his chin. Oh, he has no idea how easy that will be now that he's with me again. "And I want you to embrace your own talent. Whatever makes it easiest for you."

Caleb beams at me. "I'm done letting anyone else's fears rule me," he promises. Then he winks. "Besides, many people would say I won the lottery for ending up with a famous rock star."

"Would you?" I ask, picking up my cocktail.

Caleb shrugs. "Nah. I won the lottery by having a boyfriend who came back and faced his fears, and waited for me to be ready."

"You're worth it," I promise. Then I sigh happily as I stand up and return my favorite guitar to its place on the wall—but I don't think it will stay up there for long from now on. "I do have to explain to you some stuff about paparazzi and Google. Maybe I'll ask Roxy for help with that…"

Caleb grins. "I'll bring a notebook around with me so I don't get bored while I'm waiting for you to autograph everyone's butts."

I have to put my cocktail down as I laugh so hard that tears come to my eyes. Every time I'm close to stopping, I take one look at his great big grin and I start laughing again.

How the hell did I luck into finding this guy?

When I finally manage to keep a straight face, Caleb smiles at me. "And I've made a decision, too." He draws a deep breath, finishes his cocktail, and takes my hands. "I'm going to become a pro, too. Maybe not a full-time poet, but I'll treat it professionally. I didn't become an accountant without training and practice, so I'm going to treat my poetry just as seriously."

Before he's even done speaking, I'm standing up and hauling him to his feet. "*Yes!*" I whisper and grab him by the waist, spinning him around in a quick circle.

Caleb giggles and presses his face into my shoulder. "But that's for later. For now, there's only one more thing I need."

"Mmhmm?" I sway our bodies together gently, pulling back to look into his eyes.

"Bring me to bed, Tag," Caleb murmurs, smiling shyly up at me. "Please."

And I can't wait. Anything he wants, he gets—always.

29

CALEB

Of course we can't sneak in the door without Queenie coming to investigate. The click of nails across hardwood is the only brief warning, and then a furry body slams into my legs as the room fills with barking.

"Queenie!" Tag groans. "Where are your manners?"

But she's wagging so hard that her whole body waves back and forth, grinning up at me as she pants excitedly.

"Hello there," I greet her, dropping to my knees and lunging for her. If I hug her first and get my face past hers, she can't lick me. It works—she whines happily, but she can't reach my face to slobber over me.

Finally I manage to pull myself to my feet with a little laugh.

"There you go. He's home now," Tag promises Queenie softly. "Go to bed." He coaxes her to her dog bed with some treats and scratches while I watch on, smiling like crazy.

He's right: I'm home now. And I'm never going to leave again.

"Come on. Let's head up to bed while we're alone," Tag tells me.

I bite my lip playfully and lead the way upstairs. "Hopefully we have long enough."

Tag grins. "We've got a good hour until the stove starts to cool off. Then the heat-seeking canine will arrive."

"I'd like to say that won't be enough time, but..." I mutter with a rueful grin.

Tag chuckles and pinches my butt, making me scramble up the last few steps with a yelp. "Don't worry. We're going to get a lot of practice this winter."

"Hey," I scold him with a little slap at his hands, but they're rising to push the door open and steer me through it. He grips my shoulders, hauling me close to him.

"Can't keep my hands off you. Come here," Tag whispers, his palms igniting rough lines of fire as they glide from my shoulders to the sides of my neck. It sends shivers of delight through me.

There's so much left to explore, and I barely even know what I like yet. A whole lifetime worth of lessons to learn about myself.

Tag gently holds my cheeks between his hands, gazing at me through the dark bedroom as his thumbs stroke my cheekbones.

"Kiss me," I whisper when I can't stand the tension any longer. "Please."

He instantly leans in, crossing the scarce few inches separating us. His lips are warm, but his kiss isn't gentle or slow. It's bruising and desperate.

I moan and tilt my head back, clutching Tag's shoulders as his hands slide to the back of my head. His fingers tangle in my curls and pull them tight into fists. At the same moment, his teeth close over my lower lip, scraping them in a hot, possessive display.

"Yes," I moan, my knees going weak.

Tag's hands push at my clothes, trembling as he impatiently strips me bare. I love the cool air touching my skin, feeling vulnerable and open to all of his advances.

Then it's his turn. I can barely keep up with his impatient movements as I try to help him strip. He ends up grabbing my shoulder and hopping on one leg as he peels his last sock off.

"Don't fall over," I giggle, but the same eagerness makes my chest swell.

It feels like I can breathe Tag in and hold him in my lungs, and everything will be all right.

He finally manages to throw the sock across the room and turns back to me, grabbing my waist and hauling me into him for a fierce kiss.

I whimper as I stumble off-balance, but he takes my weight without flinching—and then I'm pressed against Tag from head to toe with nothing in the way.

The kiss is quick to deepen with need. Tag pushes his tongue against mine, and suddenly we're kissing open-mouthed in filthy and delicious motions as I rock against him.

God, it's incredible. Every inch of skin where he's touching me tingles. My hands ache with the need to explore his bare skin, so when I catch my balance, I let them run down to his chest and pinch his nipples.

"Fuck," Tag sharply pulls his head away from the kiss, his voice a sharp rough thing.

I catch my breath and freeze. "Are you okay?"

"*Good*," Tag grunts. "Do that again."

Relief floods me and eases my chest, so I grin and do it again, this time scraping my fingernails along the tiny, hard nubs as Tag grunts and pushes into me.

Our hard-ons grind together, trapped between our hard stomachs. Every time he twitches or drags against my length, sparks fly through my field of vision.

"Come here," Tag mumbles against my mouth, nipping my lips again. He pulls me over to the bed and then turns around so the backs of my knees press against it.

I giggle and take hold of his hands, then flop onto my back on the bed. I awkwardly squirm backward onto the bed with my elbows, hauling him down with me.

"Whoa!" Tag crashes on top of me but I laugh, wrapping my legs around his waist.

"Gotcha," I whisper and press my lips into his neck.

Tag finally frees his hands from mine, bracing his arms on

either side of my head. The beam of moonlight pouring through the window catches him in the light, his eyes deep wells of love.

Then he leans over to flick on the lamp, and I half-close my eyes. It's not too bright, mercifully.

"Let me see what I've got," he murmurs.

I blush and take the chance to wriggle the rest of the way up the bed, until my head rests on the pillows. I'm alight under his gaze, curling my toes into the bed.

Tag comes to me hands-first, his palms running up my naked body from hips all the way to my shoulders. Then he straddles me, his cock heavy and swollen with need. It bumps mine again and I whimper.

Tag notices. "You like that?" He grins, wrapping his big hand around both of our cocks.

"Tag!" I cry out, flailing at his shoulders and grabbing them, digging my nails in.

I wasn't expecting the sheer intensity of the wildfire that shoots straight to my core as the hard heat of him drags along my sensitive skin. Finally, I gasp for breath and manage a nod. "Just a little."

"Wow," Tag whispers. He bites his lower lip, watching me like a predator preparing for his feast. And I won't lie, it turns me on.

"Fuckfuckfuck," I whimper helplessly as he squeezes his fingers around my cock, crushing it against his shaft and stroking us both at once.

My legs slip from his waist and tangle with his, and he leans down to press his mouth on mine in a hot crush. Heat coils in my belly, far too immediate for my liking.

"Not yet," I beg. "Please."

Tag chuckles and lets go of us both. I ride the wave of disappointment, reminding myself that I'll get to feel even better soon.

"What did you want to do instead?"

My breath catches. I shiver with the tingles that spread through my body. "I'm ready," I whisper. I need him deep inside me, completing every last missing piece of me.

Tag's eyes flick wide open for a moment, like he's not quite sure what I'm asking. Or he doesn't dare to hope.

"Make love to me," I tell him. Then I grin. "And/or fuck me. I'm not choosy. Both?"

A grin creases Tag's gorgeous face. "Are you sure?"

"*Duh*," I whisper and grin up at him.

Tag laughs softly and brushes the backs of his knuckles against my cheek. "My beautiful boyfriend," he murmurs, his voice tinged with awe. "I'd be honored."

He leans over toward the bedside table, but I grab his arm to stop him. "No condom," I tell him. Then I hesitate. "I assume… it's still just been us?"

Tag chuckles in a soft, affectionate breath. He leans down to press his lips against my forehead. "Oh, Caleb. From the moment I saw you, it was just you."

"Good," I whisper and beam up at him. I want to feel him inside me without anything in the way. Not because it proves our love or anything. It's just really fucking hot.

Tag raises an amused brow. "I still need lube, though. Or I'd recommend it. Some guys can get away without it, after practice—"

"Oh. Right," I squeak. As I let go of his arm, Tag laughs richly and I join in the giggle. "Good thing I have you to show me the ropes."

"The ropes?" Tag pretends to stare at me.

"I can't say *anything*, can I? Naughty man." I groan and roll my head back against the pillow.

He only leans down to take advantage and nip my throat, flushing me with a pleasurable heat. "I am. But I'm your naughty man."

"I know," I whisper, smiling to myself while Tag finally grabs a bottle of lube from the bedside drawer.

He turns it upside-down and squirts the clear jelly over his fingers as I swallow hard. This is going to be an entirely new experience. I'm a little nervous, but at the same time I can't wait.

Every other new experience so far has been even better than I'd hoped.

"You know, you didn't send me that video," I tease. It might be kind of hot if we watched that while he gets me ready.

Instead, Tag looks crestfallen. "Oh, no," he murmurs, setting aside the lube. "I deleted it. It didn't feel right to keep it when I thought we were… you know."

"Kaput," I murmur with a wry smile as he nods. God, he's such a good guy. How could I ever have thought that he was trying to take advantage of me?

I push myself up on my elbows, grabbing the back of his head and hauling him in for a kiss. "Thank you," I murmur.

Tag makes a surprised little noise and then chuckles. "You're welcome?" He looks puzzled as I flop back against the bed. "But it was your first time and everything… I should have sent it over…"

"Don't worry about it," I tell him simply and stroke my finger up his thigh toward his cock. Then I gently flick the head of his dick, watching it bob and stand up straight again as he grunts. "The fun was in knowing the camera was on anyway. We'll just have to recreate it."

Then I lick my lips pointedly, shifting my gaze back up to his eyes.

"You tease," Tag growls softly. He shakes his head as he pushes my thighs up and apart.

I grin and spread my legs eagerly, pressing my heels almost against my butt.

The cool sensation of liquid against my entrance makes me flinch and giggle with surprise. Then he leans down to suck the head of my cock into his mouth.

"Ohhh," I groan, reaching down to grab his shoulders. It's the strangest feeling, the heat of his mouth around me at the same time as… the heat of his finger stretching me open.

He takes it slowly, but it burns in the weirdest way. Sweat beads my forehead, and it's all I can do to gulp and focus on the pleasurable flicks of his tongue around my head and along my slit.

It's almost too much sensation at once, and my brain is starting to overload.

But then, as he pushes a second finger inside, arousal rushes back all of a sudden to dominate my thoughts. I can't wait for it to be his cock instead.

My breath is heavy as prickles of pleasure build up deep inside with every stroke of his fingers. He's definitely found my prostate now. Like he has all night, Tag takes his time to tease me with fingers and tongue alike.

It's just a hint of what's to come, yet I'm already desperate for more. I swipe my hand over my forehead and clutch the pillows under me, arching off the bed to thrust into his mouth.

When I lower myself back down, it pushes Tag's fingers deeper into me. For a moment it's pleasurable, but I'm too overwhelmed to keep up any kind of rhythm.

I'm happy to let him take control—as long as he hurries up.

"Now," I moan, tapping his shoulder frantically. "If you keep that up…"

The wet pop of his mouth freeing itself from my hard cock is delicious to my ears. "Mmhmm?"

Looking down at my boyfriend is the hottest sight of my life. My needy cock jumps against my stomach.

Tag's smile is half-hidden in his short beard. Then I notice a string of precum joining his lip and my dick, just before he licks the droplet from the tip of my shaft. Then he winks at me.

My whole body surges and throbs, and it takes all I have to clench down on the wave of pleasure. I am *not* going to come before he's even inside me!

"Fuck," I groan raggedly as I collapse against the bed again. *"Please."*

"Yes, my love," Tag murmurs, and his fingers slide out of me.

My thighs quiver as I catch my breath and grunt with the

unpleasant emptiness. How did that sensation change so quickly from discomfort to desperation?

"Almost there," Tag soothes me gently. He kisses one upraised knee, then pushes my legs apart again so he can lie flat between them.

I fucking love watching him add lube to his palm and run his fist down his shaft to slick it. But he doesn't waste time pleasuring himself. There's so much more waiting for him.

Tag shifts himself until he's braced over me, his arm pressing into the bed by my ear as his lips find mine. I whimper with surprise at the sharp taste of myself.

Tag grins at me and pulls away a little bit. "That okay?"

It sure as hell is. I hungrily arch up again, answering by seeking his lips for another kiss, so he grins and then indulges me.

"Okay," Tag whispers against my lips when I've settled into that ecstasy of making out. One hand is between us, guiding the firm heat of himself to my tip.

I quiver as I eagerly push down against him.

"If it hurts, tell me. I'll go slow."

"*More*," I grunt instead, locking my arms around his back.

Tag grins and nips my jaw. "I'll give you more," he promises.

Then he's inside, the heat of him filling me to bursting and beyond.

I cry out, pressing my feet into the bed and turning my face to the side. "Oh, fuck," I gasp. It's so much more *visceral* than I'd even expected. So blissful and intimate and...

Real. Raw. *Right*.

Tag holds still until I'm squirming for more again, and then slides inside gently, inch by inch. He keeps pausing to stroke my cheek and kiss my lips and whisper about how well I'm doing.

I drink it all up—the praise and the heat of him and the knowledge that I'm yielding as the man I love enters me.

It's so overwhelming that tears spring to my eyes, but when Tag looks concerned, I grab his hip so he can't pull away again.

"I love this," I whisper, my voice faint.

He lets out a quiet breath and presses his lips to my cheek. "So do I. You're so tight. Fuck, it feels incredible."

I can't help clenching around him, my body squeezing tight in answer to his words, and Tag gasps and grunts sharply. I love seeing his reactions as pleasure floods me, too.

We're together in a way we've never been before.

I'm stretching out to fit him perfectly. The initial burn has faded to an ever-present warm tingle, and before long I find it easier to breathe and relax.

"There we go," Tag whispers, kissing my throat with open-mouthed flicks of his tongue that add notes of pleasure to the symphony playing in my body.

Time ceases to matter. All that's important is that we're here, together, and we're never going to be parted. I want this to last forever.

There's no space for layers or disguises or masks. No room to hide from each other when we're locked together, our bodies and souls becoming one.

Every thrust ignites that spot deep inside me, and before long I'm moaning and whimpering with every thrust. Every wet sound, grunt, and growled breath just drives me on. I quiver and squeeze around Tag, kneading his shoulders and dragging my nails down his back.

"My love," Tag groans. "Oh, my love." He presses our foreheads together, his skin shining with the exertion. Every heavy breath brings us one second closer to the end.

As hard as I'm trying to hold back, I'm just quivering on the edge of my self-control. "Yes!" is the only word in my vocabulary pretty soon, punctuated by my gasps and cries, which only spur him on.

Don't stop. Don't ever stop!

And he doesn't.

Tag pounds into me hard and fast, pouring every ounce of his devotion into the rhythm. Best of all, he kisses me like the world is ending… or like the future is starting.

Then the walls seem to close in around me, and the sparks break through to my tightly held-back bliss. I come undone around and under Tag, and in his arms.

My heartbeat pounds like a drum and I part my lips as I cry out, arching off the bed and pressing into him. "Yes! Tag!"

Uncontrollable heat pours from me and I buck into Tag as my cries slip free, mingling with his. I squeeze tight around him, and moments later the rhythm of his thrusts stutters. He grunts, clutches me tight, and cries out my name.

Together we ride the surge of release, all thought disappearing in the face of pure physical pleasure.

Complete together, in each other, at last.

It seems like forever before I can catch my breath and collapse on the bed again, sweaty and exhausted and utterly satiated. The euphoria tingles through my fingertips and toes, and sinks into my bones as a lazy heat.

"Mmm," Tag groans at last as we clutch each other tightly and offer up soft kisses in between trying to catch our breaths. "How'd I get so lucky?"

I giggle softly and stroke his hair. "By showing me the man you are." I press my cheek against his shoulder, running my hand slowly down his back. "I'm sorry other people didn't love you the way you deserved… but I'm glad that I get to."

Tag swallows hard and rests his forehead on my shoulder, and my heart feels so full with this fragile moment. I hold him close as he murmurs, "I'm glad, too."

We can be ourselves with each other, and that's the greatest gift I could ever want.

"Tag Campbell or Titus Taylor, I don't care what you're called," I tell him. "You were worth waiting for."

He sweeps my curls away from my forehead with one quick gesture and leans in for another long, slow kiss. It's only when we pull apart that I realize how damn tired I am.

Tag cleans us up and turns out the light, pulls back the covers and helps me underneath. Good thing. I'd probably curl up and sleep right here.

In the darkness and nestled together under the quilt, we fit together perfectly.

Just as we're drifting to sleep, the door creaks open. I chuckle sleepily, but I'm too tired to even say anything aloud.

I don't need to. Moments later, my legs are weighed down by the third member of our little family. I'm so happy that I could cry —or just close my eyes and drift into blissful ecstasy, so I do that instead.

I've found my true melody, my heart's rhythm, and my home.

30

CALEB

Eight Months Later

A quiet yelp catches my attention. I struggle to sit up from my lazy little nest: a couple of pillows in the back of the truck with a notepad and pen.

I prop myself up on an elbow and shade my eyes against the hot July sun, peering at the bee yard. The truck's parked a few hundred feet away, so that Queenie doesn't get excited and try to join in as Tag checks his hives.

"You okay?" I call out. My raised voice, of course, makes Queenie bark. Tag works slowly and cautiously, so he doesn't get stung often. When he does, I hate that there's not much I can do besides try to kiss him better.

"It's all right," Tag calls out a moment later. "I just have company in here."

I shiver and shake my head. He bought me a bee suit, so I went up close and personal—once. I saw how peaceful and gentle they are, and that was enough for me.

I'm happy to drink the proceeds. And it might not seem like it, but I'm actually hard at work on my own part in this. As he works on harvesting the honey that will go into a batch of mead, it's my job to write a haiku that will go on the bottles.

Every batch has a limited-edition, numbered haiku on the label in small print. Some people in Burlington have gotten really into collecting them.

Queenie whines from the ground on the other side of the truck bed. I lever myself over the side to check on her. She's holding a stick up for me to throw, so I chuckle and lean as far down as I can, just barely able to grab it from her.

She tries to hold on and play tug-of-war with a playful growl, but I yelp. "Let go," I order her before she can pull me right over the side. She does, dancing on her toes and waiting for me to throw the stick, so I hurl it overhead as far as I can and then fold my arm on the edge of the truck, resting my chin on it to look over the meadows.

Yeah. This is the life.

Tag is like a whole different man, totally open and relaxed about his past. Nobody seemed surprised when word got around. They'd already guessed he must have money to open a meadery from scratch.

Tourists sometimes spot him and get excited, but the locals never let Tag's ego get too big. They rib him when he plays guitar at open nights sometimes, and I think he likes it.

That's exactly the speed he wants: no money or fame, just making people happy with music and mead.

And me? Well, I'm working as an accountant, but I just got back from a writing workshop in Maine. I was glad to get home to the house we now share, and I'm doing another poetry class online.

If Tag isn't in front of the mic, I am. I do readings all the time, and I submit my poetry, and I shrug off everyone's opinions with a polite smile.

It's a beautiful life together, and when I get afraid that the happiness we've found in each other can't last… well, I just have to look at the last six months.

Sure, we fight about socks on the floor and whether drinking green tea is a redeemable quality, but it's all with love. There's no more secrets anymore.

"Hey, come look at this."

I shake myself out of my thoughts, put down my notebook, and slide out of the truck bed onto the ground.

Tag has flipped back the mesh hood of his beekeeper's suit. "Is it a trick? Are you transferring your bee friend to me?" I call out with a wary look.

Tag laughs. "No," he promises. "But if you come look at this, I'll let you brush me off and check for bees."

"Oooh." I dance up to him with a playful grin. "That's a deal." Before I can start unzipping him, he laughs and pulls away, grabbing my hand.

"Come first," he orders.

"You know I love it when you tell me that," I tease him, bumping his hip with mine and giggling as he leads me through the long, green grasses.

The beehives are tucked up against a little patch of dappled woodland. I've never been into it, but he picks his way through the trees, leading me in.

I can't help stopping to stare around at the light streaming through the soft green branches. "I should have brought my notebook," I whisper.

"Wait until you see this."

I look down again and then gasp. It's a little clearing with a fairy circle—a ring of mushrooms. Right in the middle is a stump.

Tag steps over the line into the circle and I gasp, clutching at his arm. "Tag!"

"What?" Tag blinks at me.

"God." I keep hold of his hand and step over the line, too, squinting. Nothing happens, of course. But it could have. "You need me to look after you, I swear. You're going to get kidnapped."

"How do you know we're not already somewhere else?" He grins, tugging me in for a kiss.

I peck his lips and then pull back, eyeing him. I know him. He's up to something. "If you're coming on to me, we could have put Queenie on the leash first."

Tag laughs and shakes his head, but something catches my eye. The stump is old and dead, hollowed out in the middle. And there's a shape that stands out.

I pull away from Tag and bend over, my fingers closing around the little wooden box. Someone's forgotten or hidden it here. Or I'm about to find a gift from the fairies, and I'm not sure what the protocol is on that.

"Look, I—" But the words die on my lips.

Tag is on his knee, gazing up at me with a huge smile. "Open it," he whispers.

My hands start trembling as my throat closes up. I can barely get the catch open, but somehow I manage it.

And then I stare down at the ring set against a black pillow inside. A thin line of rose gold is set just off-center in mottled silver.

When I look at Tag again, my eyes are filling with wetness.

So are his.

"Caleb Holt," he whispers. "You've already made the happiest man alive. So would you do me the biggest honor of my life, and make me an honest man at last?" He draws a breath and takes my other hand—the one that isn't clutching the ring box and trembling like mad. "Will you marry me?"

The squeal I let out startles a flock of little birds right out of the trees. I fling my arms around Tag and throw myself at him so hard that we both collapse onto the ground, and then Tag starts laughing.

"Don't lose the ring!"

"Shit," I mumble, visions of metal-detecting dancing in my head. But when I fumble for the box and raise it aloft, pointing down at us, it's still wedged tightly into its pillow. "No, it's there!"

Tag laughs and pushes us both until we sit upright. "Is that a yes?"

I almost can't speak. The earnest look on his face just cuts straight to my heart. He's always this attentive every time he looks at me... but this time, I can see a whole lifetime of these looks on his face.

"It's a deal," I manage, my voice trembling into a little giggle. As he starts to grin, I clear my throat. "Yes. Yes, Tag, *God*, yes."

Tag grabs the box and pulls out the ring, pushes it onto my finger, and hauls me down to the ground again to kiss the hell out of me.

Before I can compose myself, another tongue joins the party with a series of excited barks.

"Queenie!" I groan, but Tag laughs as she snorts in his ear.

"She can't help it. She wants to be part of it."

"Oh, she'll be our ring bearer," I promise with a grin.

Tag starts laughing. "That won't go wrong at all."

I grin mischievously at him. Secretly, I can't wait to find out *how* wrong it goes. "No, I'm sure she'll be good as gold."

She's sprawling on her back in the dirt, yelping happily at us.

"Our firstborn is dirty and needs a bath again," I inform Tag with a shake of my head. "And you want more?" He mentioned last week, in one of his less subtle moments, that the nearby elementary school had a good music program.

He grins at me. "Well, we haven't screwed up too badly, apart from her love of the dirt."

"We'll see," I promise him with a wink.

For now, it's just the two of us.

I like it that way.

I have to brag to everyone I know and then celebrate this development all weekend long. But first, I have to keep touching the ring, rubbing my fingertip against it.

"There's a melody etched inside," Tag finally murmurs as he takes my hand.

I yank my hand away. "I'm not looking. Not yet. You can take it off and show me on our wedding day, Tag."

He just laughs that beautiful rich laugh of his and kisses me, surrendering as usual.

As Queenie explores the clearing and finds another stick to chew, we curl up together. We could spend hours this way, watching honeybees investigating the little flowers that carpet the forest floor.

It's prettier than even a poem. I couldn't hope to try to capture the joy of the moment—though I'm certainly going to keep trying in the years to come.

For now, words fail me. All I can do is kiss him and breathe in this simple joy: together at last, forever.

THE
END